Jack and Noah's Big Day

The Summer When Everything Happened Just Like No One Had Imagined

Jay P. Slagle

DEDICATION

To Jeana, Jack, Greta and Henry.
You are my life's adventure.

CONTENTS

INTRODUCTION

When two 8-year-old boys decided to make their summer vacation more interesting, their parents didn't give it a second thought. But that was before their neighborhood was upset by police cars, television reporters and a warning from the County Health Department. Individually, those things and maybe even the elephants, exploding house or slushie machine might not have been news. But when all this happened in one summer, in one neighborhood, there had to be something, or someone, seriously crazy.

1 PRINCESS DRESSES – MONDAY, JUNE 9

The day started quietly enough. Jack Taylor, his 7-year-old sister Greta, and his 5-year-old brother Henry had been out of St. Margaret Mary's school for two weeks. The swimming pool had been open for exactly four perfect days before the temperatures rose and summer storms rolled into Omaha. Jack used the remote to change the TV to the Weather Channel. He'd learned how to do that by watching his Nana, who lived across the street and was always watching for bad weather. The TV said that it was going to continue to rain pretty much non-stop for the next week, just like it had for the past five days. Jack's backyard had already turned into a lake, and Jack wished he hadn't given away his plastic fishing pole.

"Mooooooommmmmmm," Jack cried out. Silence.

"Mooooooommmmmmm."

Again, no answer.

Jack climbed up the basement stairs and yelled again. Still no answer, but he thought he heard his mom's hair dryer. He clomped up another flight of stairs and found his mom, bending over in the bathroom doing something weird to her hair. It kind of looked like her head was on backwards. Or upside down.

"Mom, it's never going to stop raining. What are we going to do for fun this week?"

His mom twisted her head back on the right way and turned off the hair dryer. "You can't run because of your beak?"

"No, Mom, I'm bored. It's going to rain all week. What are we going to do for fun?"

"Well," his mother replied, "we're serving dinner at the homeless shelter tonight, but that's about all we're doing this week. What sounds fun to you?"

"I think we should stick with something simple. Maybe just go to Disney World for a few days, or fly to California, because the Weather Channel says it's not raining there, or maybe we could just go buy new toys at the toy store. If it's going to rain all week, we're definitely going to need new toys to keep us out of your hair."

"Jack, I…," his mother paused.

"OK, if you don't like those ideas, I say we go car shopping. I saw on TV that we can buy a new car that has two video screens for watching movies, and you can even watch real TV on them while the car is moving. That would make the drive to church that much faster."

"Jack, we don't need to fly to Disney World or California just because it's raining, and we certainly don't need to buy new toys to have fun. We also don't need a new car. Our van is great, it takes us less than five minutes to get to church, and you already watch too much TV. Anyway, there are lots of fun things to do in Omaha even if it's raining. There's bowling, the zoo, the Children's Museum, PlayDaze, and yesterday I bought some paint to work on an art project."

Jack considered the options in his mind. In the last two weeks he'd done all of those 'fun' things except painting, and no one would mistake him for Picasso, who his mom said was a famous painter from two million years ago. He frowned back at his mom. "That all sounds boring. How about we just invite Noah over instead?"

Jack's mother scratched her head, which was still on the right way. Raising three children had taught her many things, but this was one of her most important truths. If it's going to be raining all day, inviting a friend over is the best way to stop a whining kid. She handed Jack the phone as quickly as she could.

Greta and Henry also invited friends, and then five neighbors arrived at the back door, so by 11:00 there were wall-to-wall kids in the Taylor house. Eleven children, all under the age of 10, and perfectly content as long as nobody touched one another, said something rude, or picked up a toy that someone else had ignored for the last hour. In short, it was really, really loud.

The center of chaos was the basement, where the carpet was rapidly drowning in toys as play boxes were emptied one after another. When Greta and Mary began dressing the youngest boys in Disney princess dresses, Jack whispered to Noah. They quietly snuck up the stairs.

Stella the basset hound was keeping watch at the top of the stairs. Well, keeping watch is a bit of an exaggeration. Stella was passed out cold. Stella liked to sleep until 10:00 in the morning, but she had been awakened early today because Greta had the ability to scream at the same frequency of a dog whistle, silent to human ears, but torture for hounds. Jack and Noah tiptoed around Stella, being careful not to trip over her ears.

They continued up to the second floor, and then finally up to the third-floor attic where they wouldn't be found for at least ten minutes.

"OK, Noah, the princess dress-up game is the last straw. Our baseball season is over next week, and we need something fun to do for the rest of the summer. We can only swim for two hours a day, so that leaves us like, what, twenty-two hours to fill each day?"

Noah had a thoughtful look on his face. "Well, we probably ought to squeeze in some sleeping time. And my mom makes me read every day. And we have to eat, and watch cartoons, and go to church on Sundays."

"OK, OK, I see your point. It's not twenty-two hours," Jack paused, "but I figure we've got at least six hours a day where we've got nothing, absolutely nothing, to do. You know there's no way our moms will let us play video games that long each day."

Noah nodded in agreement. "And if it keeps raining, then swimming won't be an option either. We need that one thing that my mom always talks about. It's called, um, a distraction?"

"No, you mean a decimal. That's what my dad says when Greta's music is too loud, 'too many decimals, turn it down!'"

"But that's it!" Noah shouted. "We need something to keep us decimated from being bored. So what can we do?"

"Well, yesterday I looked at our calendar," Jack said, "and we have eleven weeks before we go back to school. My birthday, August 18, is ten weeks from today. We have to do all the school shopping and haircutting stuff the last week before school. So that means we've got ten weeks, seven days a week, six hours a day…"

Noah interrupted, "That's like ten thousand hours of contraction! We need to find something huge to do. Like really huge. Bigger than the 4th of July huge!"

"What would be bigger than the 4th of July?"

"The 5th of July?"

"No, that's not it. How about we build our own car?" asked Jack, as he tilted his head upwards and dreamed about a magical car with two TV screens.

"We don't know a thing about building cars. We do know how to play baseball. Let's go play for the New York Yankees for the rest of the summer. We'd be on TV and famous and all that stuff!"

"Nah, I don't want to live in New York all summer. I'd miss my mom's cookies."

"Speaking of food, I'm hungry." Noah's eyes glazed over as he dreamed of pancakes with syrup and whipped cream.

Jack ignored Noah's stomach. "Let's build a huge roller coaster in our backyard!"

"Jack, your backyard is way too small. It would have to be in my backyard, but my mom planted a garden this year, so I'm sure she would veto that idea."

"What's blotto?"

"That's when you have a great idea but your parents won't let you do it. They veto it. The President of the United States vetoes stuff all the time."

Both boys stopped talking. Jack scratched his chin, because his dad once told him that scratching his chin helped him think up good ideas. Noah rubbed his stomach. He was still hungry.

Neither boy said anything for at least five minutes, which generally only happened when they were asleep or getting the evil eye from their moms. Jack suddenly jumped up and said, "I'm going to the bathroom."

The bathroom door was right next to the wall where the boys had been sitting. Jack closed the door, but immediately began talking.

"We need to find something to do that is totally giantnormus, but doesn't sound giantnormus to our parents. They will snotto any idea that sounds giantnormus."

"Jack, my mom said I'm not supposed to talk to people in the bathroom. She never lets me talk to her when she's in the bathroom. She calls it her 'alone time.'"

"I'm not going to the bathroom. My Grandpa Phil used to say that he did his best thinking in the bathroom. I've never tried this before, but Grandpa Phil had all kinds of crazy ideas."

"Are you sitting on the toilet?"

"Where else can you sit in a bathroom? Anyway, the lid is down, so stop weirding out and start thinking giantnormus."

Five more minutes passed. No talking.

"Jack, this whole thinking up ideas in the bathroom is dumb. At this rate, you'll be in there until your birthday in August. Come out…"

Before Noah could finish his sentence, he heard a commotion in the bathroom and Jack flung open the door. Unfortunately, the door swung back and smacked Jack on his right kneecap. There was a loud thunk, the kneecap yelled bloody murder, and then Noah heard a series of thuds and rattles as various parts of Jack fell to the floor and rolled around like a jar of loose change. Noah stepped into the bathroom doorway and looked down at Jack, now lying on the bathroom floor. Jack was holding his right leg and making grumpy faces. However, Jack's left leg was shaking like it had been invited to a one-leg lay-on-the-floor dance contest, and in between his grumpy faces he looked excited.

Jack began to grunt-talk through his pain: "I know… ugh… what to do… ow…, I know what … oof… to do!" He got to his feet, and tried to stand up straight. Jack was breathing hard and a little line of sweat had formed over his upper lip. He stumbled over to a chair and collapsed into it. The one-leg dance contest was still on.

"Let's plan ... the coolest birthday party ever for me... and invite all of our friends... and we'll spend all summer planning it. Maybe... we'll even invite girls... so everyone knows about it when school starts again."

"Girls? Are you serious?" Noah looked like he was going to get sick.

"OK, no girls, except maybe moms... but only if they help at the party. No little sisters, no neighbors, no classmates, no girls at all."

"Absolutely. Let's plan a boy birthday party. If our birthday party had girls, there's no way it would be the coolest birthday party ever."

"I can't wait to tell my parents. They're going to love this idea."

2 MONEY PROBLEMS – TUESDAY, JUNE 10

Eight-year-old Jack didn't much like to eat, and he was always running somewhere. He viewed food as an enemy, or at least food that was nutritious. He loved spaghetti without sauce, plain rice, bread and popsicles. He liked pizza, one kind of meat (pot roast), one vegetable (steamed carrots, never raw ones) and no fruit. Mrs. Taylor had resorted to making carrot and pot roast pizza.

The school nurse once sent home a letter that said Jack was so skinny he was invisible sideways, and so she recommended he never twist right or left or he might be permanently lost. His parents didn't need the letter to realize that. Jack's pants never seemed long enough and he was always getting holes in the knees, forcing Mrs. Taylor to sign Jack up for the Pant-of-the-Month club. On about the fifteenth of each month, the mailman delivered a new pair of pants one-half inch longer than the previous month's pair. Greta and Henry were jealous about this arrangement, and begged Mrs. Taylor to sign them up for the Doll-of-the-Month and Video-Game-of-the-Month clubs. She refused.

Jack smiled a lot. His teeth were big and bright, and he had his mother's freckles below his eyes and across his nose. Over the past year he'd gone from a buzz cut to long, thick hair that kept falling into his eyes. A ponytail couldn't be far away.

Jack had bright hazel eyes, but the most striking thing about them wasn't their color. His eyes captured everything around him. He noticed license plates, momentary frowns, new house decorations, even missing signs along a busy street. In first grade, it was Jack who noticed that the pizza slices served on the fourth Wednesday of every month at school were getting a little bit smaller each time. He wrote a complaint letter to the school board. Mr. Taylor said the school board lived in Macademia, a very small African country that Jack could never find on a map.

Anyway, after receiving Jack's letter, the school board promptly launched an investigation and discovered that for several years the lunch lady had indeed been making smaller pizzas, reducing the size a little bit every month. She then used the extra dough, mozzarella cheese and tomato sauce to make a ten-foot high sculpture of her cat. The lunch lady was immediately fired and Jack was given an extra recess for tipping off the school board. The half-completed cat sculpture now sat in the lunch-lady's front yard as a gathering place for birds, squirrels and various insects that had no taste buds.

Noah and Jack met in kindergarten. That was practically three years ago, when they didn't know how to read, write cursive, or catch a baseball. They were buddies almost immediately, drawn to sports and games and whatever seemed funny at the time.

Like Jack, Noah was the oldest kid in his family, which meant that he did as much work around the house as his mom and dad. Mr. Patton worked at a construction company, which was possibly the coolest job ever, so Mr. Patton played with bulldozers and dump trucks every summer day while Noah stayed home to clean toilets and pick up clothes off the floor. Noah figured he'd be doing the family's grocery shopping before long.

Noah had a mop of light-brown hair. His mom had meant to cut it for Easter in April, but Noah ran faster than the barber. In fact, despite being one of the shorter boys in the second grade, Noah was one of the fastest. He was a hockey player too, and he seemed to scoot rather than take full strides, but it worked for him.

By Tuesday night, June 10, the rain finally cleared long enough for the Sun Devils to play a baseball game. Jack and Noah both pitched an inning and the Sun Devils' bats were on fire. They defeated the Angels 10 to 3, improving their record to fifteen wins and three losses. Their three losses had all been against the Red Sox and Yankees – the two teams in the major leagues that hated each other. Sadly, the second loss against the Red Sox had knocked the Sun Devils out of the running for the league championship. The Sun Devils were now just playing for fun. That was fine with Jack and Noah.

After the game, Jack and Noah grabbed their bat bags and rushed over to their waiting parents. "Mom, Dad," they yelled in unison, "we need to have a meeting." The two sets of parents started laughing.

"Since when do you boys hold meetings?" asked Mrs. Taylor.

Noah ignored the question and looked at his parents. "Mom, Dad, Jack and I were talking yesterday, and we have way too much time on our hands this summer. We need something big to do, a contraption, so that we don't have to bother you all the time."

"We were thinking…" Jack started, but was interrupted by Noah.

"We were thinking that we'd like to start our own zoo, beginning with a giraffe and a tiger."

"Never going to happen," said Mr. Patton.

Noah looked defeated, his shattered dreams lying in the grass. Jack tried again. "Well, then we want to build a motorcycle ramp in Noah's backyard."

"Not a chance," chirped Mrs. Taylor.

"Flying lessons?"

"Oh, no. Not in my lifetime."

"Hike around the world?"

"Only if the world ends a block from our house."

"Make our own fireworks?"

"Out of the question," said all four parents in perfect unison.

"Fine. If you're not going to let us do anything fun, then we want to plan a big party in August for my birthday."

"Since when do you plan parties, Jack?" asked his mother.

Noah answered before Jack could. "If we have a party to plan, then we wouldn't be bugging you guys all summer long. But we'll have to spend a lot of time – I mean a lot of time – together."

Noah's mom needed some convincing. "So how are you going to pay for this big party that takes all summer to plan?"

"I've got $478 in my bank account plus another $80 in my wallet, and you told Noah that he has over $500 in his savings account," replied Jack, very proud that he remembered the exact dollar amounts. "And we're going to need all of it to pay for the elephant and clowns and bounce house and motorcycle stunt dude."

"Slow down, buddy," said Noah's dad. "Noah's $500 is for college, not a big party. Besides, I'm pretty sure that your dad isn't going to let you hire a motorcycle stunt dude with your $500."

"It's actually $558, Mr. Patton," Jack replied, and then he turned to his parents. "Come on, Dad, I can have the motorcycle guy, right?"

"Jack, here's two dollars. You and Noah go to the snack shack and we'll discuss it while you're gone."

After the boys walked away, the parents began talking.

Mrs. Taylor went first. "Can you believe they want to spend over $500 on a party? Jack's party last year cost less than forty dollars, and he had a great time with ten of his friends."

"At this rate," Mr. Taylor noted, "he'll be asking to borrow my car when he's nine."

"Spending that kind of money is crazy," Mrs. Patton noted, "but Noah does have a lot of time on his hands this summer. I didn't sign him up for any camps, and we have to stay close to home because of Meredith's naps." Meredith was Noah's one-year-old sister, just learning to walk, and she required two naps a day. If Meredith missed a nap, she got pretty mean.

Mrs. Taylor nodded in agreement. "We're not doing camps either; our favorite one got cancelled because not enough families registered. Really, it's not like anything big will come out of their party planning. Maybe this will keep them occupied for a few weeks until they find something else to do. What's the worst that can happen when they're always in sight?"

Mr. Taylor, who never liked to spend money, had the final word. "Let's tell them that we'll give Jack $50 for his party, and that's all they get. And," Mr. Taylor paused for a moment, looking at Mr. Patton, "I want to be clear that the elephant needs to go in your back yard. I have a hard enough time cleaning up after a dog."

When Jack and Noah returned from the snack shack, Mr. Taylor gave them the news. Noah, fresh off the starring role in the second-grade play, clutched his chest when he heard about the $50 limit. He staggered, groaned, stumbled, gasped, and eventually ended up as a lump on the ground. Jack was a bit less emotional.

"FIFTY DOLLARS? ARE YOU KIDDING ME? HOW CAN I HAVE THE COOLEST BIRTHDAY PARTY EVER FOR $50?"

"After that little yelling fit, you're down to $45, Mister," Mrs. Taylor said quite sternly, and Jack knew he needed to dig out of trouble quickly. "We make the rules, and you can either accept them or forgot about planning the party."

"I'm sorry, Mom, I'm just… well… disappointed, I guess." Jack already knew what a $40 party was like, and he doubted the extra $5 would make it the world's coolest party.

"Can I use my allowance money, too? You always say that I never spend my allowance money on anything fun, so I'd like to spend my allowance money for the next ten weeks on the party. That would be ten weeks, $8 allowance per week, so another eighty…"

His mom cut him off with a shushing sound. "You still have to give $3 to church every week, Jack, so don't be counting that money. But," and she thought for a little bit, "yes, we will let you spend the other $50 of allowance money on your party."

"With that $50, we're up to $95. How much of my allowance money do I get to spend?" asked Noah.

Mr. Patton answered. "Noah, this is Jack's birthday, so you two only get to spend his money. Your money is off limits."

"On the bright side," Mrs. Patton said cheerfully, "we have agreed to let you be together for two hours every weekday, starting at 9:00. After two weeks, we'll decide if you've had enough of each other."

That was the first bit of positive news the boys had heard. Jack usually only saw Noah a couple of times a week, and now he could see him five days a week.

With the discussion over, the Taylors and the Pattons collected their chairs and belongings, and walked from the baseball field to their cars. Jack and Noah walked slowly, well behind the adults.

"How can we plan the coolest birthday ever for $95?" asked Noah.

Jack shook his head. "I have no idea. We may not even have enough for balloons, and you can't have the coolest party ever without balloons."

"Or elephants."

3 CONFLICT – WEDNESDAY, JUNE 11

The next morning Jack ran down the stairs promptly at 8:00.
Stella lay sleeping at the bottom of the stairs, but she took the
energy to open one of her eyes as Jack passed. Jack always spent a
few minutes each morning trading slobbers with Stella – it's
impossible to trade civilized kisses when Stella's tongue and jowls
are so big – but today he ran straight into the kitchen. His dad
was usually at work by now, but he could hear his parents talking
in the kitchen.

After trading hugs with each of his parents, Jack got straight to
the point.

"Mom, Dad, I've been thinking about our party a lot."

"When you say 'a lot,' you mean…"

"You know, A LOT. I woke up at 7:45 today, and I've been
thinking about it since I got up."

"So for fifteen whole minutes," replied his mom. "And what have you been thinking?"

"I think – and so does Noah – that $95 won't be enough to have the coolest birthday party ever."

His dad laughed. "So, on the coolness scale, does $95 get you 'great,' 'good,' 'below average,' 'embarrassing' or 'worst party ever?'

"I think it's probably going to be stuck between 'embarrassing' and 'worst party ever."

"Jack, you're frustrating me," and his mom wasn't laughing. "We've never spent that much money on one of your birthday parties, and you're still complaining. I've never seen you be so selfish. Maybe we should cancel this whole idea."

"Sorry, sorry, sorry, …." but then Jack paused.

Above the kitchen, Jack and his parents could hear quick footsteps, and then they got louder as Henry reached the wooden stairs. Clomp, clomp, clomp he went down the twenty stairs to the first floor. Henry yelled, "Aww, Stella," and Jack could hear Stella and Henry snorting while they rolled on the ground together. A few moments later, Henry entered the kitchen, the left side of his face glistening from Stella's greetings.

"Good morning, Henry," said Mr. Taylor.

Henry just grunted, which was about all Henry did in the morning. Henry needed more sleep than anyone in the family because he was five and because he played harder than any kid Jack had ever seen. Part of the problem was that Henry thought he had to keep up with Jack and do everything Jack did, which was a bit hard since Henry wasn't much taller than a fire hydrant. Henry skipped the hugs, grabbed the TV remote control, and climbed onto his stool at the breakfast bar. Henry needed his morning cartoons like adults needed their first cup of coffee.

Jack turned back to his parents. "I'm sorry, Mom. Please don't cancel the party. I do appreciate the $95 but... but I was thinking..."

"I was thinking, too," said Henry. "I want to have the coolest birthday party ever this summer."

"You can't, Henry," replied Jack. "Your birthday isn't until December."

"Then I want the coolest half-birthday party ever."

"Henry, we don't celebrate half-birthdays."

"Maybe we should start. I always have to have my birthday party indoors, and Jack can have it inside or outside, and he gets elephants and motorcycle dudes, and all I usually get is a cake. Plus, last year we gave all my party presents to that homeless shelter."

"Jack is not getting an elephant for his birthday." Mrs. Taylor seemed very sure about this. "And you already had sixteen presents from your grandparents."

Just then, Greta appeared in the kitchen. Even though she had just rolled out of bed, her long blond hair looked like a movie star's. "If Jack has an elephant for his birthday, I want one for my next party too."

Mrs. Taylor threw her hands up in the air and appeared to whisper something to someone above the ceiling. She lowered her head and looked at Greta. "Jack is not having an elephant at his party. He can't afford an elephant, there just aren't elephants waiting to be invited to parties, and, by the way, elephants step on little kids. THERE WILL BE NO ELEPHANTS!"

"That's fine," said Greta. "But if Jack gets a motorcycle dude for his birthday, then I'm having one at mine."

"Jack is not having a motorcycle dude at his party. If Jack did have a motorcycle dude at his party, you'd get to see it then. The three of you don't need a motorcycle dude at every one of your parties. I can't believe we're talking about motorcycle dudes," Mr. Taylor said as he collected his backpack so he could go to work and escape this conversation. Mrs. Taylor asked if she could please go with him, and they both started to leave the kitchen.

"Greta won't see the motorcycle dude at my party. She's not invited."

Both Mr. and Mrs. Taylor stopped at the kitchen door and turned back to Jack. "Excuse me?" said Mrs. Taylor, in her you're-in-big-trouble voice. "Did you just say that Greta's not invited to your birthday party?"

"Noah and I decided that it's a party just for boys in our grade. No girls except maybe you and Noah's mom, and no little kids."

"So I might be invited, but Greta and Henry are out of luck?" Mrs. Taylor had just grown a bunch of wrinkles on her forehead, and her smile was…. well, gone.

"We're going to have mature entertainment, Mom," Jack explained, "and we decided that it wouldn't be as fun with girls or little kids. I'm sure they wouldn't have fun anyway."

Henry was getting angry, and he pointed a finger coated in powdered donut sugar at Jack. "Oh, yeah, I would never have fun at a mature party where there are motorcycle dudes and elephants." He jumped off his bar stool and stomped upstairs to his bedroom.

"THERE WILL BE NO ELEPHANTS AT THIS PARTY!" Mrs. Taylor seemed to be getting mad. She didn't usually yell in capital letters.

Greta wasn't much happier. Turning to Jack, she said, "I didn't know that girls would ruin the coolest birthday party ever. I'll have to remember to not invite girls to my next party." Greta, who hadn't even started her breakfast, stomped upstairs to her bedroom.

Mr. and Mrs. Taylor were both frowning now. Mr. Taylor had his backpack on his shoulder, and without saying anything, he stomped to the back door and left for work. Jack had always thought that 'stomp' was a fun word, but not anymore.

"Well, now that you've made everyone mad," Mrs. Taylor said, "you can finish your breakfast. While you're sitting there alone, I hope you realize how badly you're acting." She paused. "Noah will be here in thirty minutes for your first planning session. Your party idea is not starting off well."

Jack had to agree.

4 THE LIST– WEDNESDAY, JUNE 11

Noah arrived promptly at 9:00 a.m. Mrs. Taylor, who usually was really happy, didn't even say 'hi' to Noah when she opened the front door. She walked past him and went to the Patton's car to talk to Mrs. Patton.

"What's up with your mom, Jack?" Noah asked.

"Oh, it's no big deal. There are just a few birthday party ideas she didn't like."

"Nothing big, right?"

"No, no, we're fine. She's not real excited about the elephant, and the motorcycle dude, and not inviting girls or little kids, but she'll probably change her mind. She only yelled in capital letters about the elephant."

"My mom got pretty mad too when I said that Lauren and Meredith couldn't come to the party. I tried to explain to her that girls ruin parties, but she didn't seem to understand. Parents can be so frustrating sometimes."

The boys walked up to the attic, and immediately began setting up an office. They hung a "Do Not Disturb" sign on the attic door, but it didn't work very well. Henry, who was just learning to read, thought the sign said "Donuts," so he came into the attic looking for something to eat. Noah sent Henry away and changed the sign to "Private." Henry thought that meant the boys were playing pirates, so he returned with a sword and eye patch. The next sign, "Confidential," looked like 'dentist' to Henry, so he asked for a free toothbrush and a sticker. Finally, Jack changed the sign to "Keep Out." The new sign, and a warning from Mrs. Taylor, kept Henry and Greta out of the way for the rest of the morning.

"So," began Noah, "how can we plan the world's coolest birthday party if we only have $95?"

"It's going to be hard, but maybe an elephant doesn't cost that much to rent. Plus, my mom has always said that I can talk adults into doing just about anything, so all we have to do is find a motorcycle dude, and I'm sure he won't even charge us."

They settled into their chairs. Noah pulled a waffle out his back pocket and a bottle of syrup from his backpack. The waffle was a bit chewy and the syrup kept getting on his fingers, so he couldn't talk for a few minutes. Jack went down two flights of stairs to find a pencil. Then he went back downstairs to sharpen it. After that, Noah realized that they didn't have any paper in the attic, so he had to go get that. While he was downstairs, he grabbed a stapler, two paper clips, a dozen cookies and a telephone. In movies, people in offices were always talking on the phone, so their office needed one just in case someone important called.

After all this, Jack wrote "Party Ideas" in big cursive letters at the top of a blank piece of paper. They stared at it for at least ten minutes.

Mrs. Taylor interrupted them when she came upstairs with a snack. Noah hid the second waffle he'd just pulled out of his pocket. "So how is the party planning coming? Do you have any great ideas yet?" She set down two Rice Krispie treats and noticed the mostly blank piece of paper. "Well, that's a nice heading you've got there. If you're stuck, maybe you should write down every idea you have, and decide later what's a good or bad idea."

"That's brilliant, Mom. I'm going to the bathroom."

"Jack, we don't announce when we're going to the bathroom."

"It's OK, Mrs. Taylor. He's not going to the bathroom. He's thinking in the bathroom."

Mrs. Taylor rolled her eyes and walked downstairs, muttering, "I always knew Grandpa Phil was a bad influence…"

With Jack in the bathroom and Noah sitting at the desk, the boys did more thinking than they had the entire previous week. By 11:00 a.m., they had the following list:

<u>*Party Ideas!!*</u>

1. Elephant rides
2. Motorcycle stunt dude
3. Target practice with bazookas
4. Clowns, but not scary-looking ones
5. Octopus wrestling
6. Bounce house
7. Bull fighting
8. Water balloons
9. World's largest soccer game
10. Burping contest
11. Tie-dye shirt making
12. ~~Kissing booth~~
13. Climb the tallest building in Omaha
14. Jump off the tallest building in Omaha (land on a bunch of mattresses)
15. Face painting
16. NASCAR race cars
17. Parachute from airplanes
18. Turtle races
19. Homemade fireworks show
20. Screaming competition

"This is an amazing list, Jack. Our parents are absolutely going to love it."

"Totally. I know my mom was mad about not inviting girls and little kids, but when she sees this list, she won't even care about that anymore."

"I bet your dad will love octopus wrestling, and my mom loves fireworks shows."

"Great work, Noah. This party planning stuff is a piece of cake."

"Your mom made cake? I'm starving."

📖 📖 📖 📖 📖 📖 📖 📖

Jack and Noah each shared the list with their parents that night at dinner. Mr. and Mrs. Taylor didn't talk for a long time after they read it. Jack could see that they were thinking hard. They also kept making weird faces at each other, but they were trying to be sneaky about it.

Finally his mom said, "Wow, Jack, that's an amazing list. I think your dad is going to say some pretty important things now. Right, Honey?"

His dad began coughing, and some steak and mashed potatoes shot out of his mouth, flying just over Jack's shoulder. Stella, sound asleep on the floor behind Jack's chair, caught the food in her mouth in mid-air without opening her eyes. She licked her lips twice and resumed her snoring.

Jack could tell that his dad wasn't quite prepared to say anything smart about the list. His dad took a long time to finish chewing the food that had managed to stay in his mouth. Finally he put down his fork.

"Well, Jack, we said that you could plan your party however you wanted, but you probably don't have enough money to do all these things. I really don't know how much, for example, a non-scary looking clown would cost. Plus, there seem to be a few things on the list that might be illegal for 8-year-olds. In fact, a few of these would be illegal for an adult to do. I must say I'm surprised that you left 'driving a tank' off your list."

"We discussed it, Dad," replied Jack, "but tanks go too slow. They're just not exciting enough for our birthday party."

"I'm curious about this octopus wrestling," added Mrs. Taylor. "Will you be doing that in water, where you can't breathe, or out of water, where the octopus can't breathe?"

"Obviously, Mom, it's going to have to be in the water. Have you ever seen an octopus outside the water? We're just going to have to wear scuba diving gear when we wrestle. It's really very simple."

Mr. and Mrs. Taylor raised their eyebrows at each other.

"Jack, it sounds like you've got this all figured out. Maybe Mom and I can help you figure out which items on your list are safe, and then you can find out how much each of them will cost."

Jack smiled. He had expected his dad to say that everything on the list was a bad idea. He certainly didn't expect his dad to help with the party.

After dinner, Jack invited his parents to the party headquarters in the attic. He only had two chairs, though, so his dad had to sit in front of Jack's desk on a stack of pillows. The stack of pillows was a little shaky, so Mr. Taylor fell off the stack, knocking over Mrs. Taylor and her chair. Mrs. Taylor landed on the waffle that Noah had hidden (and forgotten) earlier that morning. The waffle, and its very sticky syrup, became attached to Mrs. Taylor's head. Stella appeared at the top of the attic stairs, sniffed at the waffle on Mrs. Taylor's head, and returned to her bed on the first floor. Stella refused to eat food that wasn't fresh.

Mr. and Mrs. Taylor returned to their pillows and chair. Mrs. Taylor quickly picked out the activities that would not be allowed. Since the party was going to be in their back yard, there was no room for a motorcycle stunt dude, even one with a really small motorcycle. The NASCAR race cars were kicked out because Mr. Taylor was sure they would be racing somewhere else that weekend. The third strike was parachuting from an airplane; Mrs. Taylor said that Jack couldn't do that until he was 70.

"I also have a real problem with jumping off the tallest building in Omaha," said Mr. Taylor. "I believe Omaha's tallest building has at least 40 floors."

"Relax, Dad. We're going to stack a couple of mattresses at the bottom."

"And you think that's going to be safe enough?" Mr. Taylor looked skeptical, as he fell off the pillows again.

"I jump from the top bunk bed onto a bean bag chair all the time, and I never get hurt. Just give me a few weeks, and I'll have it all figured out."

Mr. and Mrs. Taylor gave Jack suggestions about the things that they didn't cross off the list. His mom had a friend who worked at the zoo, so she would call about the elephant rides. His dad would call The Amazing Arthur, a semi-crazy magician, to see if he knew any non-scary clowns. Mrs. Taylor gave Jack the phone number for a rental store to find out the cost of a bounce house. Jack and Noah had to figure out the rest of the ideas on their own.

His parents got up to leave, but his dad paused just before he went down the stairs.

"Jack, I'd like you to reconsider the kissing booth. I see it's crossed off your list, but it's one of my favorites. Maybe Mom could be in the booth…"

"Stop it, Dad…"

"And you could sell tickets…"

"You're grossing me out…"

"And I'd buy at least one hundred of them…"

"Eeyuck…"

"I'd bring some Chapstick for my lips," added Mrs. Taylor.

"I'm going to get sick!"

"And maybe we could have that cute little Mary Beth from your school be in the booth for you," added Mr. Taylor.

"Dad! Absolutely not!"

Mr. and Mrs. Taylor laughed all the way to the kitchen.

5 LITTLE SISTERS – THURSDAY, JUNE 12

Jack went to Noah's house the next morning at 9:00. His SpongeBob SquarePants backpack was full of pens and blank paper just in case they had a lot of good ideas that day. Noah and Jack hurried to Noah's room and locked the door. Lauren, Noah's five-year-old sister, started knocking almost immediately. When they didn't answer, she laid on the ground and talked to them underneath the door.

"I'm bored, Noah. Play with me."

"Get lost, Lauren. We're having an important meeting."

"What's a neeting?"

"Go away, Lauren. We're busy."

Noah started the meeting. "My parents said that we can't sky dive, race cars or have the motorcycle guy at the party."

Jack shook his head in disbelief. "My parents said the same thing. Can you believe they think so much alike?"

"Yeah, what are the chances that two sets of parents would cross out exactly the same things?"

Despite their disappointment, the boys still had sixteen ideas on their list. At 9:15, Noah's mom knocked on the door and handed the phone to Noah. He said 'hello,' grunted 'uh-huh' several times, and then hung up with a sad look on his face.

"That was your mom, Jack. She talked to her friend at the zoo, and they don't rent elephants. In fact, he's never heard of anyone ever renting an elephant, but he says that he will let her know if he finds someone who does."

Jack threw a stuffed animal across the room. The elephant rides had been first on his list because that was what he wanted most. He had been sure that you could rent anything these days, including an elephant.

Noah continued on. "Your dad also talked to The Amazing Arthur. Arthur says a scary clown will be about $150 for an hour, but a non-scary clown will cost at least $200. Arthur said he will do an hour of magic tricks for $100 if we let him ride the elephant."

Jack threw his hands in the air and sighed loudly. "And I called the rental store, and a super-large bounce house costs $250 for one day. So right now, with $95, we can't even afford to rent a scary clown, and even if we did, we wouldn't have any money left for water balloons, face paint or ice cream." He paused for nearly a minute.

"Noah?"

"What?"

"I think the first thing we need to do is earn more money."

"And how do we do that?" Noah asked.

There was another knock on the door. Lauren called out, "Noah, I'm still bored. Will you please play with me? Mom says she has work to do."

Noah rolled his eyes and looked at Jack. Jack had a huge grin on his face.

Noah was annoyed. "What's so funny? Doesn't your little brother bug you all the time too? I always have to entertain her when my mom is busy."

"I know, and your babysitting talent is going to make us some money. Noah, starting next week we are going to hold 'Jack and Noah's Summer Camp' every Tuesday. I can see the poster now: 'Send your children to camp for two hours, and they'll thank you for a lifetime.'"

"Our summer camp is going to be the memory of a lifetime?"

"Hey, if a kid is only five, how many good memories can he have?"

Noah smiled. Jack was right. Running a summer camp would be easy.

6 APPROVAL – THURSDAY, JUNE 12

Mrs. Patton was crawling on the bathroom floor when Noah and Jack found her. The boys weren't actually looking for her. Their plan had been to do some serious thinking about the summer camp in the bathroom, since Jack had already proven that he got his best ideas there. However, since Mrs. Patton was cleaning the toilet – which made Jack wonder, for the first time in his life, how often a toilet is supposed to be cleaned – they decided to talk to her.

"Mom, we've been thinking."

"That's good, Noah. Eight-year-olds rarely spend much time thinking, especially during the summer. Thinking is good."

"We've been thinking about the $95 we have, and how the coolest birthday party ever is probably going to cost more than $95."

"Noah, there is no way that you and Jack are going to use your college money for a party."

"I know, but…." Noah paused. "But what if we did extra work this summer and earned money for the party."

"Noah, we were very clear that you couldn't use your allowance for the party, and any work you do around the house is in return for your allowance. Do you think you're going to go out and get a job? Do you know how many people can't find jobs right now?"

"Mrs. Patton, we know that it's hard to find a job, even for two really smart and good-looking kids like us." Jack and Noah gave Mrs. Patton their best angel smiles. "But if we did find a job for the summer, could we spend the money we make on the party?"

"Sure, Jack. If you find a job, and if it's safe for eight-year-olds to do the job, and if you actually get paid for the job, then sure, you can use that money for your party."

"Thanks, Mom, you're the greatest."

"Noah," Mrs. Patton said as she wiped off the toilet one last time, "you need to aim better."

7 ADVERTISING – FRIDAY, JUNE 13

Noah was in charge of creating a poster to advertise the summer camp. He didn't want to do it, but he and Jack agreed that it was the job of whomever had the higher grade in handwriting. In addition, Noah had a way bigger box of markers than Jack. It took Noah nearly all of Wednesday and Thursday afternoon to complete it, and his brain was tired from spelling.

Jack and Noah's Summer Camp

When: Every Tuesday morning, 9 - 11 AM

Where: The Taylor house on 52nd Street

What: Fun, games, art projects, story time, singing contests

Who: Open to all kids 3 - 7; must be potty-trained. No brats.

How much: $4 per kid per day

Jack's mom is in charge of big problems

Your kid deserves the memory of a lifetime at
Jack and Noah's Summer Camp.

Jack's dad charged the boys $3 to make 100 copies of the poster on bright green paper at his office. Then on Friday evening, Noah and Jack rode bikes with their dads around their neighborhoods. They left the posters at every house where little kids lived.

After they were done, they realized that the poster didn't include a phone number for moms to make reservations. They decided that they couldn't waste $3 more on new posters, so they would have to wait until Tuesday to see if they would have any campers. They figured that five kids would equal $20, and if they held camp for eight Tuesdays before the coolest party ever, they would have $160 more to spend.

Jack and Noah lived about a mile apart but pretty much in the same neighborhood. They were both surrounded by dozens of families whose kids also went to their school, and the neighbors talked to each other a lot. Jack and Noah didn't know it at the time, but their summer camp was the talk of neighborhood mothers the entire weekend.

8 OPENING DAY – TUESDAY, JUNE 17

On Tuesday morning, June 17, Noah arrived at Jack's house at 8:30 to prepare for any kids that might appear. Lauren came too, along with her $4 camp fee. Henry and Greta were also going to be at the camp, but they got in for free because Mrs. Taylor said so.

Just before the 9:00 start of camp, the boys made a pitcher of lemonade for the mid-camp snack. Their first camper, Luke, arrived at the back door at 8:55. Luke was a four-year-old who lived behind the Taylor's, and he was the little kid in the neighborhood who was always in some sort of trouble. Because of this, everyone called him Crazy Luke. Crazy Luke liked to climb trees, sit on the roof of his mom's car, run in the middle of busy streets, and chase squirrels. In some ways, he was more of a dog than Stella. However, Crazy Luke's biggest problem was that he loved firecrackers, and he loved to throw firecrackers at the feet of adults who weren't expecting the big bang that followed. Crazy Luke's dad thought this was funny, so he made sure Crazy Luke always had a good supply of firecrackers.

Jack rolled his eyes at Noah when Crazy Luke arrived.

"Four dollars is not enough to babysit Crazy Luke," he whispered to Noah.

"No kidding, Jack. One hundred dollars might not be enough, but we're stuck with him. Let's see if anyone else comes."

Noah and Jack grabbed the list of camp activities they had prepared the day before and ran to the front door to welcome campers. Hopefully they'd get at least one mom to stop if they sat on the front porch.

Jack unlocked the front door and gasped, so Noah ducked his head under Jack's outstretched arm. He gasped even louder than Jack. There were a dozen kids already running in the front yard. A row of at least eight minivans was illegally parked on 52nd Street, waiting to drop off kids. They were definitely going to beat their goal of five campers.

Jack volunteered to stand on the front porch to collect money and write down the name of each camper. The kids then walked straight through his house to the backyard, where Noah quickly lost control of the kids on the swing set. Greta and Lauren just laughed as Crazy Luke and another little kid tried to tie up Noah with a jump rope. Greta was only seven, but she knew way more about babysitting little kids than Noah.

At 9:30, kids finally stopped arriving at the front door, and Jack ran to the backyard. By then, Noah was firmly tied to a pole on the swing set, and a group of little boys were chanting in a circle around him. If there had been a big pot in the backyard, Noah would have been boiled by then.

Balls were flying in the air and a three-year-old was shooting water from the garden hose on anyone near him. Three little girls were chasing Stella around the backyard, which was unfortunate. Stella mostly liked to eat and sleep, and running wasn't anywhere on her "Top Ten Favorite Things to Do" list.

It was really, really loud.

Jack untied Noah, and they tried to start the games on their list. 'Duck, duck, goose' didn't hold the campers' interests, and a game of freeze tag ended up being a game of tackle football, with Jack's stolen baseball hat being used as the football. Noah suggested a game of dodge ball, but after five minutes the campers were only throwing the ball at Jack and Noah. Every game on Jack and Noah's list ended in disaster, and there were still forty-five minutes before camp was over.

In a panic, Jack brought out the lemonade. The pitcher was quickly emptied, and the campers began chanting. "More drink, you stink, more drink, you stink…" Jack and Noah kept making lemonade, but the chants started again as soon as the pitcher was empty. Jack grabbed four boxes of Oreos from the basement, along with every other kid snack in the house that he could find. Finally, at 10:45 the chanting stopped, and the campers grew quiet.

"It took a while, Noah, but I think we're getting the hang of this. They're finally behaving." The boys were standing at the back door, watching the campers sitting in the backyard.

"Jack, why are they all looking up? Why are they pointing?"

The campers got excited again, and began chanting, "Luke, Luke, Luke…"

Jack and Noah ran to the middle of the backyard and looked up. On the top of the house, sitting near the edge of the third-story roof, sat four-year-old Crazy Luke. He was happy. Jack and Noah were not.

Jack, Noah and Mrs. Taylor ran to the attic and tried to convince Crazy Luke to climb back through the window he had used to reach the roof. Crazy Luke was having too much fun and would not budge. The chants continued. The fire department was called.

Three fire trucks arrived just before 11:00, followed by a row of mothers in minivans. Crazy Luke was rescued by two large firemen who could barely squeeze through the attic window. The fire department had recently begun charging a fee to rescue cats from trees and rooftops, and the fire chief decided that Crazy Luke wasn't much larger than a cat and certainly as annoying. The chief handed Mrs. Taylor a $100 invoice as he left the house.

The last kid departed at 11:15. No one had gotten hurt or lost, and most of the campers left begging their moms to bring them back next week. Some moms even gave Jack a few extra dollars because their kids had so much fun.

After they finished picking up all the toys in the backyard, the boys dumped all the money they had collected onto the kitchen table. They had to count it three times because they couldn't believe the total amount was correct.

"Jack, we have $156 here. We already have enough for a non-scary clown!"

"Hold on, Noah," said Mrs. Taylor. "Have you counted your expenses?"

"Oh, I forgot. Yes, $3 for the 100 posters we made."

"You went through four cans of lemonade, so that's another $10. How many boxes of Oreo's did they eat, Jack?"

"Four."

"That's another $16. What other snacks did you use?"

"A box of chocolate chip cookies, a box of Rice Krispie treats, some fruit roll-ups, a bag of candy bars, two boxes of graham crackers, a loaf of bread, a jar of peanut butter, three tomatoes, a can of whipped cream, and two gallons of ice cream."

"Tomatoes?"

"We thought they wanted to eat them, but it ended up that they wanted to throw them at us. By the way, I have a few stains on my shirt."

"OK, I'm just going to guess that's another $30."

Noah was busy writing all of this down. "That's $59 dollars of expenses. Take that away from our $156, and we made $97 dollars today."

"Until you pay the $100 fire department charge. I wasn't in charge of Luke today. You two were."

"So our profit is…"

"A negative three dollars. I was tied to a swing set, had tomatoes and balls thrown at me, listened to forty kids yell at me for two hours, and after all that – we lost three dollars." Noah's chin fell to his chest.

"How can we have a job and lose money?" asked Jack.

"You don't have a job," said Mrs. Taylor. "You have a business, and right now business is bad. Very, very bad."

9 NO HELP – WEDNESDAY, JUNE 18

Noah and Jack spent the next morning trying to solve their camp problems. They needed to do some serious thinking, so Jack moved to the attic bathroom as soon as Noah arrived. Unfortunately, Noah needed to use the bathroom for something other than thinking. Jack left the bathroom for a few minutes. When he returned, he discovered that bathrooms are not good thinking places when they smell badly. He retreated from the bathroom, closed the door, and shared the desk with Noah for the remainder of the meeting.

The boys had to improve the camp. New moms had discovered Jack's phone number and had been calling every night since the first camp, so the boys were pretty sure their second camp would be bigger than the first.

The biggest problem with more kids was that Jack and Noah didn't know how to control them. They had tried to play all the games they remembered from when they were little kids, but the campers didn't like the games, didn't follow directions, and didn't listen to a thing that the boys said. It reminded Jack of a substitute teacher who couldn't control a class, except Jack and Noah couldn't threaten to take away recess if the kids didn't behave. The camp was a two-hour recess.

The boys were out of ideas. They were desperate. They had no other options. They had to go to their moms for advice.

"Mom," said Jack, while he was eating lunch after Wednesday's meeting with Noah, "Noah and I are trying to figure out how to have camp go better next week."

"Go better? You mean you didn't plan the fire trucks? The moms I've seen said that the fire trucks were the highlight of the camp for their kids." Mrs. Taylor thought for a few seconds. "Maybe next time you could plan a tornado or hurricane."

"Mom, we can't have a hurricane in Nebraska. Please be serious. The campers don't listen to us, and we can't afford to lose more money. We need to make money if we want to have the coolest party ever."

"Jack, you've had babysitters. Think of the best ones, and why you liked them."

"They played what I wanted to play, and they listened to my stories, and they were funny. They acted like their job was to make sure I had fun."

"With those forty kids yesterday, did you do all of those things? Did you listen to them and play what they wanted to play? Was your job to make sure they had fun, or were you focused on how much money you were going to make?"

"Geez, Mom, it's kind of hard to listen to forty kids when there's only two of us. So… oh, I get it, Mom. We need more help. We'll get you and Mrs. Patton and…"

"Jack, this is your business, not mine, and it's for your birthday party, not mine. If you want to have a successful camp, you need to do it without my help."

10 DELEGATION – THURSDAY, JUNE 19

When Jack and Noah met the next day, they spent most of the time calling people so they could be prepared by the following Tuesday, June 24. One problem they noticed at the first camp was that Jack's backyard was too small. Jack negotiated with Delaney, another 8-year-old who lived next door, to rent her very large backyard for $10 every Tuesday. He also convinced her to become their very first volunteer camp counselor, and he put Delaney and Greta in charge of organizing each week's activities. Unfortunately, Greta wasn't interested.

"Greta, this is an important job. You should be honored that I asked you," Jack explained.

"I should be honored that you asked me to volunteer at your camp, so you can make money, so you can throw the coolest birthday party which, by the way, you're not going to let me attend? Holy cow, Jack, I AM SO HONORED!"

Jack needed Greta. When little kids came over to Jack's house, Jack always ignored them, but Greta would have them playing house or dolls or whatever. Lauren and Henry, and even Crazy Luke, always listened to Greta.

"OK, Greta, you can come to the party."

"Lauren gets to come too."

"Fine."

"And Delaney and her little sister."

"Fine."

"And five of my best friends. I will give you a list of them one week before the party. My best friend list changes too often to give you the list now. Do you agree to my terms?"

"Fine." Jack had no choice. She could have asked to bring every girl she had ever met, and he would have had to say 'yes.' Jack and Greta shook hands on their agreement, and she dismissed him from her room.

Even after adding Delaney's backyard, Jack still needed more space for the camp. The Douglas family lived behind the Taylor house, and you got to their backyard by going through a secret gate behind Jack's garage. Mike Douglas was nine years old and too old for camp, but he agreed to rent his backyard to Jack for $5.

Mike had a real talent for making up songs, so Noah suggested that Mike write a song for camp. When Jack asked Mike to be in charge of teaching camp songs every week, Mike was so happy he almost jumped out of his shoes. It took about ten seconds for Jack to talk Mike into being a volunteer counselor too. This was good, because Mike was also Crazy Luke's older brother, and Jack hoped that having Mike at camp might prevent another visit from the fire department.

Even with Greta, Delaney and Mike as counselors, the boys still felt like they needed more help, but they didn't want to pay anyone. Their friend, Joey, had an older brother and sister, Jacob and Rachel, who wanted to break into the babysitting business. Noah and Jack offered to let Jacob and Rachel hand out their babysitting posters to the moms at camp if they became camp volunteers.

The boys also decided they needed entertainment. Noah heard about a fifth-grade neighbor who had been practicing to be a magician for almost a whole year. Because Fletch Johnson was so excited to perform in front of someone other than his relatives, Noah didn't have to offer Fletch the $6 that he had intended to pay him. However, one entertainer wasn't enough for Noah.

Noah's mom was walking one morning in Memorial Park, a few days after the first camp, when she saw a grandpa training two golden retrievers to perform tricks. She told Noah about the dogs and the grandpa, who happened to live a few blocks away. Noah went to visit him, and the grandpa, Mr. Sullivan, thought a bunch of loud kids would prepare his dogs for the pressure of dog shows, so he agreed to come every week too.

Jack acquired the talents of Ralph, a high school soccer player who could play basketball using only his head and feet. He could dribble the ball, make perfect passes, and sink shots into Jack's basketball hoop from thirty feet down the driveway – without using his hands. His final trick every week would be to have campers throw balls at his head, and he would bounce them into the basket. Jack negotiated his toughest agreement with Ralph; a six-pack of Mountain Dew and headache medicine after every show.

11 SUCCESS, SORT OF – TUESDAY, JUNE 24

The day of the second camp arrived. Jack and Noah felt prepared, but they had also felt that way before the first camp when things didn't turn out well. Six pitchers of lemonade were waiting in the kitchen, and Mrs. Taylor had bought two large jars of animal crackers for snacks. Jack had spent an hour at the grocery store on Saturday and had decided that animal crackers were the cheapest snack food they could buy.

In addition to Greta's new responsibility for planning activities, Jack also put her in charge of registration. Campers would come to the front porch every Tuesday, and then Greta would write down their names while Noah and Jack collected the money.

Sixty-two kids came to the second camp, two more than Jack and Noah had predicted. All the kids were registered by 9:10, when Greta moved to the backyard to begin the activities.

Noah had told Greta to have Fletch the Magician go first, because he would get the campers' attention. Fletch did, but for all the wrong reasons – and reasons that Noah would have discovered if he had made Fletch audition. Fletch started his magic show by attempting to pull a rabbit out of a hat but, as much as he tried, he couldn't find the stuffed rabbit that was supposed to be hiding in the hat. Just before the show, Crazy Luke had taken the rabbit and fed it to Stella who, being particularly hungry that day, thought a stuffed animal would hit the spot. The campers booed Fletch and his missing rabbit.

Fletch tried a new trick. He had a camper pull a card out of a deck, and then he tried to guess the card (a three of spades). It took Fletch 35 guesses, and would have been more if Noah hadn't held up three fingers after about 20 guesses. Fletch's final act was to juggle three baseballs, but after two campers had to be given ice packs for baseball-related injuries, Jack stepped in to end the show. Fletch felt bad about his performance, so he volunteered to hang around after his magic show to help Delaney and Greta.

Mr. Sullivan and his two golden retrievers were next. While the golden retrievers were particularly well trained, Stella was not. As the retrievers went through their tricks, Stella followed along sniffing them in places that were, well, not appropriate. Stella eventually realized that Mr. Sullivan had a pocket full of dog treats that he would give his dogs when they performed a trick. After Stella tried to tackle Mr. Sullivan three times, he gave up, gave Stella all of his treats, and then tried a few magic tricks to keep the campers entertained. He was worse at magic than Fletch.

After Greta led the campers in a few games, the counselors handed out snacks, and then Ralph the soccer player started the last performance of the day. Jack had made Ralph audition, so he knew that Ralph really could kick a soccer ball into a basketball hoop from the end of the driveway. The campers "oohed" and "aahed." For his final act Ralph let the campers throw balls at his head, and he knocked them into the basket. He was perfect through the first five campers, but Ralph didn't make the sixth basket. Instead of a soccer ball, Crazy Luke threw a large rock at Ralph's head. Rocks don't bounce particularly well. An ambulance was called.

The ambulance pulled away from Jack's house just as the minivans began arriving.

Despite Fletch, Stella and Crazy Luke, the campers raved about camp as they went home with their mothers. Noah had not been tied to a play set and no one besides Ralph had been injured. Jacob and Rachel had booked four babysitting jobs by the end of camp, and they promised to bring back more volunteers next week. Jack and Noah were feeling pretty good as they sat at the Taylor's living room table counting money.

"I counted $240 dollars from the camp fees, plus one mom gave us a $10 tip," Jack said. "What are our expenses?"

"It cost $15 to rent the two extra yards, $20 for the lemonade and animal crackers, and we'll still have to pay about $10 for Ralph's headache medicine and Mountain Dew."

"By the way, Jack," his mom called from the kitchen, "Ralph just phoned from the hospital. He said his emergency room bill was $225. You can pay him next week when he comes back to camp."

Jack's face drooped about three inches. Add some long ears, and he would have looked a lot like Stella. "Noah, how much did we make?"

"Give me a minute. This subtraction stuff is pretty hard." Finally, he spoke. "A negative $20. We lost money. Again."

Jack and Noah had the most popular money-losing business in town.

📖 📖 📖 📖 📖 📖 📖 📖

Every night before bed, Jack, Greta and Henry had to tell Mr. and Mrs. Taylor their 'thanks to God' of the day. Sometimes a 'thanks to God' was a gift, like a birthday present, but more often it was playing with friends, having a good baseball game, or spending time at Nana's.

The boys were lying in bed when their parents came in to kiss them goodnight.

"Jack, what's your thanks to God for today?" asked Mrs. Taylor.

"Nothing, I guess. It sure wasn't the camp."

"What about what the mailman brought?"

"I am not wearing those pants from the Pants-of-the-Month Club. I do not wear pink!"

"Henry, Jack doesn't have any thanks to God today. How about you?"

"Swimming, camp, seeing an ambulance, basketball with Jack, chasing Stella, eating ice cream, Jack's pink pants, and being with Mommy and Daddy."

"Wow, Henry, I thought Jack did all those things too," replied Mr. Taylor. "Jack, it sounds like Henry is a lot better at counting his blessings than you are."

"I'm better than Jack at everything!"

12 NO BETTER, MUCH WORSE – WEDNESDAY, JUNE 25

Jack and Noah had lost $3 at their first camp and $20 at their second camp. They had started their party planning with $95, and they now had $72. The elephant, non-scary clowns and everything else seemed further away. As they sat in their office in Jack's attic, Noah was almost too nervous to eat the peanut butter and jelly sandwich he'd stuffed inside his sock. Jack wasn't doing well either. He was in his thinking bathroom when Noah arrived.

"Jack, I think we need to review our progress."

"Sure," Jack said through the door.

"So we've collected $406 in camp fees in two weeks. The campers love the camp. The parents love the camp. Our volunteers love helping at camp, and Jacob and Rachel are bringing more counselors next week. But..."

"But," interrupted Jack, "the only thing Fletch knows about magic is how to mess it up, and Stella attacked the dog trainer. We've had three fire trucks and an ambulance at my house, and we're losing money."

"We've definitely got an expense problem."

"We don't have an expense problem. We have a Crazy Luke problem."

"We've spent $325 for the fire truck and emergency room. If we could just find a way to keep Crazy Luke under control," Noah said, "we could be making a lot of money."

"What does Crazy Luke love more than anything, Noah?"

"Firecrackers, of course."

"How about we promise to give him money for firecrackers if he behaves?"

"That's a great idea. He'll do anything for firecrackers."

13 BRAIN FREEZE – TUESDAY, JULY 1

The third camp went much more smoothly. Jack and Noah supervised 22 counselors and performers, and practically all of them worked for free. More importantly, the camp's popularity was increasing. Greta registered 90 campers on Tuesday, July 1. She also began collecting e-mail addresses from parents, although Jack wasn't sure why.

Fletch was back for his second performance, but he had given up serious magic. Greta had searched the Internet for a listing of the most popular magic tricks, none of which Fletch could do, but Greta didn't care. Every time Fletch messed up a trick, the campers roared with laughter. Fletch was a horrible magician, but he was a pretty good comedian.

Mr. Sullivan and his golden retrievers were back, but only after Jack promised to put Stella in her kennel during their performance. Although the dogs performed perfectly, after just a few minutes the campers began chanting Stella's name. Mr. Sullivan shrugged his shoulders and nodded to Greta, who released the hound. Stella chased and sniffed the golden retrievers around the yard for a good two minutes before she collapsed in exhaustion. The campers cheered, Mr. Sullivan smiled, and Stella snored.

Mike Douglas taught the campers his newest song, "I Bake My Own Boogers," that wasn't quite as popular as last week's song, "Your Underwear is Under Where?" However, Greta had told Mike that he couldn't sing an underwear song every week, so he was doing the best he could.

Jack had talked to Crazy Luke before camp, and Crazy Luke was on his best behavior, but only because he was running low on firecrackers. Even Crazy Luke could behave once in a while.

With all the hard work given to someone else, Jack and Noah didn't have much to do once Greta started the camp activities. After they collected the money and sent all the campers into the backyard, Noah and Jack wandered down the street to get away from the noise. They ran into Mr. Brown, who was piling a bunch of junk in his front yard.

"Whatcha up to, Mr. Brown?" Jack asked, as he started a staring contest with a sad mannequin, which is basically a fake person.

"Well, we're moving next weekend into a smaller house, so I need to get rid of a bunch of this stuff. We're going to have a yard sale starting tomorrow."

They had some time to kill, and Noah saw some pretty cool things in the yard. "Mr. Brown, if we helped you carry stuff out here, would you give us a good deal if we found something we liked?"

"Absolutely," he replied. "I could sure use the help. My knees aren't what they used to be."

For the next hour the boys grunted, lifted, snorted and sweated. The last thing they carried out was a big machine with an electrical cord. It had silver metal on the bottom and two tall glass tubs sitting on top.

"What is this, Mr. Brown?" Noah asked.

"Oh, that's called a margarita machine. We used to have a lot parties, and we would make frozen drinks in them. I think you kids call them 'slushies' now – they sell those drinks at George's Gas Station. You put in some water and a big packet of something like Kool-Aid, and a few hours later you have a nice cold drink."

"How much?" Jack asked.

"Well, I suppose you would get about twenty drinks from each tub."

"No, I mean how much to buy it from you?"

"Well," Mr. Brown said, "you guys have saved me a lot of time, and I just want it out of here, so you can have it for free."

As they carried the slushie machine away, Noah looked a little confused. "Jack, why do we need a machine that makes forty drinks at a time? There's no way your mom will let you keep this in your kitchen."

"Noah, have you ever had a slushie?"

"Of course I have. They're like the best drink in the world on a hot summer day."

"Which is exactly why we're going to open 'The World-Famous Slushie Stand' next week."

📖 📖 📖 📖 📖 📖 📖 📖

Jack and Noah got back to Jack's house just as camp was finishing. Mrs. Taylor refused to let the boys bring the slushie machine into the house. In fact, she was quite insistent that the slushie machine stay outside. "Rocket engines belong in rockets, not in my house. Get that evil contraption out this second or I'll call animal control and have you boys locked in the pound!" The boys scurried out the back door, just ahead of a flying oven mitt.

After a five-minute rest to get the feeling back into their exhausted arms, they parked the machine in Mr. Taylor's garage stall. They covered the machine with a blanket and warning signs

– "Touch this and you will die" and "This is not interesting so
don't look at it." This only increased the curiosity of Henry and
Crazy Luke.

"What's that, Jack?" asked Henry, as Henry, Crazy Luke,
Greta and several other neighbors crowded around the blanketed
machine.

"It's a time machine. Mr. Brown has been hiding it in his
basement for twenty years, but he sold it to us for a thousand
dollars."

"A thousand dollars," Henry gasped, "Mom's going to kill
you! Where did you get a thousand dollars?"

"The thing is," Noah said, playing along with Jack's story and
avoiding Henry's question, "it's the only real time machine in the
world. Mr. Brown used to be a scientist, and he invented it. Go
ask him if you want."

"Mr. Brown was a scien-fast? Whoa," said Crazy Luke, who
was too little to pronounce big words very well. "Show us how it
works."

"Let's see," Jack said, as he looked around the garage. Behind
the neighbor kids, about fifteen feet from the slushie machine, he
pointed at one of Mr. Taylor's old overcoats on a pile of clothes
that Mrs. Taylor was giving away. "How about I put that coat on,
and then I'll get into the time machine and go back two minutes,
and you can see how it works."

Henry and Luke were jumping with excitement as Jack put on the overcoat, and walked to the back of the slushie machine. Noah put a finger to his mouth and said, "Quiet, it has to be quiet for this to work. This is all very dangerous."

Noah lifted up the back of the blanket, but not enough for the neighbor kids to see what was beneath it. Jack got under the blanket, and then crouched down so he was leaning over the slushie machine.

"OK, now this machine is a little old, so it's going to shake a lot. Mr. Brown said that sometimes weird things shoot straight out of it, so look at the ceiling. If you see anything, we'll have to report it to Mr. Brown immediately. OK, are you guys ready?"

Henry and Crazy Luke nodded their heads while they stared at the ceiling. Greta, Delaney and the other neighbor kids were just shaking their heads. Noah leaned over Jack and acted like he was flipping a switch. Jack made a rumbling noise, and then started shaking as he slipped off the coat.

"Look at the ceiling, I think I saw something," yelled Noah, and Henry's eyes bulged as he and Crazy Luke looked up.

Jack kept making his rumbling noise, but he lifted up the back of the blanket and handed the overcoat to Greta, who quietly placed it back on the pile of old clothes.

Noah leaned over the slushie machine and made a clicking noise. "Well, that should have been long enough, guys. I set the

time machine to go back two minutes. Let's see what happened."
He pulled up the blanket and Jack stood up, wearing his normal t-
shirt and shorts.

"Let's see," Jack said, as he looked around the garage. He
pointed at the clothes pile. "How about I put that coat on, and
then I'll get into the time machine and go back two minutes, and
you can see how it works."

Henry and Crazy Luke squealed with excitement. They both
ran out of the garage screaming, "We have a time machine! We
have a time machine!"

Sometimes having a little brother is all the fun a kid needs.

📖 📖 📖 📖 📖 📖 📖 📖

Noah called his mother, who agreed to let him stay at Jack's
house until dinnertime. After lunch, the boys temporarily moved
their headquarters to Jack's garage. They removed the blanket,
and Jack began flipping switches on the slushie machine. Noah
pulled a bruised banana out of the waistband of his shorts and
began to peel it.

"Jack, those switches aren't going to work without electricity."

"Plug it in, then, Mr. Scientist."

Noah plugged in the electrical cord, and then peered into one of the tubs while Jack flipped switches. The slushie machine parts started turning.

"Is it working?" asked Noah.

"No idea," said Jack, as he grabbed the top half of the peeled banana out of Noah's hand, and dropped it in the glass tub, "but this might tell us."

The slushie machine turned the banana into mush, and when Jack turned on the nozzle, liquid banana squirted onto the floor.

"That was my after-lunch dessert."

"That was disgusting. How can you eat a banana that has been in your shorts all morning?"

"It might have cooled me off. Why doesn't your garage have air conditioning?" Noah had beads of sweat forming on his forehead. In any group of boys, Noah always seemed to sweat the most, and he was winning this competition too.

Jack shrugged his shoulders. "Maybe we should have taken a picture of the machine, and held our meeting in the attic. Anyway, where are we going to set up our slushie stand, and how will we get customers?"

"You live on 52nd Street, and it seems kind of busy. In addition to all the cars, there sure are a lot of fire trucks and ambulances that stop on this block."

"We could have it on the corner of the block, but we'd have to run a really long power cord from my house. I wish a little kid lived in that corner house. I bet we could rent an electrical outlet from a little kid for $2 per day. There's no way an adult would agree to those terms." Jack scratched his chin again. "What about your house, Noah? You live on a quiet street, and it's pretty wide. Do you ever have fire trucks or ambulances on your street?"

"Never seen one. Plus, my garage is pretty close to the street, and my dad has an orange power cord that would reach the street."

"And your bathroom is right inside your front door. That's going to be important. One day I had two slushies and went to the bathroom sixteen times." Jack really liked to go to the bathroom.

"But if my street isn't very busy, how will anyone know we're selling slushies?" asked Noah.

"Should we do television ads? Or how about radio commercials? My Grandpa Phil always says that I have the perfect face for a job on the radio. But wait; my dad's company used to advertise on the radio, and he said you have to pay to do it. I think we need to keep our expenses low. I'll ask my dad for advice at dinner."

Henry and Greta had already finished their dinners by the time Jack talked to his dad. Jack was a slow eater and was always the last person at the table. "Jack," his dad said, "should we use your time machine so you can see what your dinner looked like when it was still hot?"

"Very funny, Dad." Jack paused. "Dad, Noah and I want to start a slushie stand. We know we can't do it in front of our house, but Noah's street hardly has any traffic. How will people know we're open?"

"Tough question, Jack. Have you thought of putting a big sign on the side of an elephant?"

"YOU'RE NOT GETTING AN ELEPHANT!" Mrs. Taylor yelled from her office.

"Dad, that's not helping."

"Maybe the wrestling octopus can use all eight tentacles to call eight different people on the phone. No, wait, that wouldn't work. People in Omaha don't speak Octoplengish."

"Thanks, Dad, you've been really helpful."

"Jack," replied Mr. Taylor, "I'm worried you already have too much going on with your summer camp. If you want to start a slushie business, you're going to have to figure it out all by yourself."

After dinner, Jack and his mom went to the grocery store. As they passed a busy intersection, Jack noticed a man holding a big sign that said, "Store Closing Sale 60% Off." On the way back home, the man was still standing there, still holding the sign. That got Jack thinking.

14 SIGN LANGUAGE – WEDNESDAY, JULY 2

Mrs. Taylor dropped off Jack and the slushie machine at Noah's house at 9:00 a.m. the next day. Jack and Noah were both excited to share the ideas they had come up with since yesterday. It took less than an hour to finish their plans.

Jack was in charge of making two large signs that said, "Ice cold slushies, $2, turn right now" and "Ice cold slushies, $2, turn left now." Mrs. Patton took the boys to Target to buy bright pink poster boards, and he wrote the words with thick, black markers. Mr. Patton stapled the posters to wooden sticks.

Noah was responsible for recruiting someone to hold the signs. Noah lived about one block away from Underwood Avenue, a pretty busy street, so he wanted two people to stand on Underwood and direct customers to Noah's house. Jack and Noah thought that Henry and Lauren would be perfect for this.

"You want Lauren and Henry to do what?" asked Mrs. Patton.

"They need to stand on Underwood Avenue for about two hours a day, holding these signs, and directing people to our house," replied Noah. "Geez, Mom, they're five-years-old. It's not like they have something more important to do than hold a sign all day."

"Five-year-olds do not stand alone on busy streets. I can't believe you suggested it." Mrs. Patton stomped off. Jack and Noah sighed. Parents sure were protective of their little kids.

After several other sign-holder suggestions were shot down by Mrs. Patton – apparently Greta, Delaney, Mike Douglas and even Crazy Luke were off limits – the boys decided that they had to get someone who was at least 12 years old. Noah called twin brothers he knew, Dirk and Turk, who agreed to hold the signs Wednesday, Thursday and Friday from 9:00 to 11:00. In return, Dirk and Turk got to play Noah's new video game for six hours per week.

Jack also designed flyers to hang on the front doors of houses close to where Noah lived. The flyers were pretty cool. Jack had his dad copy them on light pink paper, and then he cut them out in the shape of what he thought looked like a tall glass.

Is the hot morning sun tiring
you out? Come to Noah's
Slushie Stand at 657 Sunshine
Drive for a reflecting drink,
9:00 – 11:00 every Wednesday
through Friday.

Just $2 for the best
drink ever fruited.

The boys were sure the money would start rolling in next
Wednesday.

15 FINE JEWELRY – THURSDAY, JULY 3

In the midst of planning a slushie stand, the boys were also looking forward to the 4th of July celebration. Every year Omaha celebrated Independence Day with a concert at Memorial Park, a huge park a block from Noah's house, on the other side of Underwood Avenue. There was also an amazing fireworks show when it got dark. Over 25,000 people would come to the park for the concert, but the park was so large that there was still enough room for the kids to play football or race or do whatever else they wanted.

The music wasn't important to the boys. Jack's dad said that the musicians had been famous twenty years before Jack was born. Their parents would sing along with the bands. Parents could be so weird sometimes.

The boys had been coming to the celebration since they were babies, so they knew everything there was to know about it. Most importantly, they knew that there would be at least 5,000 little kids there. And little kids love glow-in-the-dark necklaces, bracelets, earrings and glasses. Jack and Noah were sure about this, because they had been little kids once.

Of all the things they had planned to do this summer, selling glow-in-the-dark things at the celebration was their oldest idea. They had come up with the idea at last year's celebration, after Jack's dad brought just enough necklaces from home for the neighbor kids. The rest of the night, little kids and parents kept asking Jack where he had bought his necklace.

On July 3, Mr. Taylor took a day of vacation to celebrate his birthday. After Jack came back from Noah's house at 11:00, Jack and his dad went to the county courthouse. Jack put on his very best manners and approached a window at the County Treasurer's Office. His dad stayed at the back of the room.

"How are you, young man?" asked the lady behind the counter. She had wrinkles and white curly hair, and she reminded Jack of grandmas he had seen on TV.

"Fine, thank you," Jack responded, and then he said very quickly and perhaps a little too loudly, "I would like to buy a peddler's license."

"How old are you, and what on earth are you going to sell?" the lady asked.

"I'm eight years old, and I want to sell glow-in-the-dark necklaces at the 4th of July party tomorrow night."

"I see. Do you have any photo identification to prove who you are?"

Jack had to think hard on that question. He opened his Spiderman wallet to look for something, but he was pretty sure he didn't have a photo ID. It's not like he needed one to drive a car or go to the bank or anything like that.

He was surprised, then, when he found last year's membership card for the amusement park where his family went every summer. The card was hard plastic, and had his name and picture on it just like a driver's license. He gave a big smile and the ID card to the grandma.

Grandma's face didn't react like Jack had expected. She looked like she was sucking on a lemon for a moment, and then she said, "Just a minute, Jack. I need to speak with my supervisor."

Moments later, Grandma came back with a very tall man with a black mustache, hardly any hair on the top of his head, and a long, sad face that reminded Jack of his basset hound. He spoke, "Son, I'm sorry, but I don't think we can accept an amusement park pass as photo identification. You probably need an adult to apply for a peddler's license."

Jack looked back at his dad, who was sitting on a bench and not being helpful in any way. Jack held up his palms as a sign

77

that he needed help, and his dad just shook his head. Mr. Taylor wasn't about to come to his rescue.

Jack turned back to Grandma and Mr. Basset Hound. "My sister reviewed the peddler's license rules on the Internet, and there's nothing there about being an adult."

"And how old is your sister?"

"Seven. But she knows the Internet pretty well. And," Jack paused as he pulled a crumpled piece of paper out of his front pocket, "these rules don't mention one thing about photo identification. The rules say that I need to give you my name, my address, and $15." Jack slid the paper across the counter to Mr. Basset Hound, which was a bit difficult, since the counter was as tall as he was.

Mr. Basset Hound took the paper and read it for a minute. He stared at Jack. Jack stared back. Mr. Basset Hound stared at Mr. Taylor. Mr. Taylor shook his head. He wasn't going to help Mr. Basset Hound either.

Greta was right. Jack didn't have to be an adult and he didn't need to prove who he was. After a bit of fussing, Grandma gave Jack a blank form, and he used his best handwriting to fill it out. After five minutes of waiting, Jack received his first peddler's license.

Once Jack had the license, Mr. Taylor called Mrs. Patton with his cell phone. Mrs. Patton was waiting at a party store to buy 600 glow-in-the-dark necklaces for $300. Noah and Jack had originally planned to buy 100 necklaces. However, they had earned over $300 from the third week of camp, and they were certain they could sell most of the necklaces.

16 THE BIG BANG – FRIDAY, JULY 4

On July 4th, the Taylors and Pattons took part in their neighborhood parade at noon. The parade was only five blocks long, but anyone who wanted to be in the parade just had to show up. Mr. Patton guessed that there were 2,000 people in the parade and only 500 people watching from the curb. Noah and Lauren decorated his bike and her wagon for the parade, and they won 1st place in a decorating contest after the parade.

A few hours later, Noah began stacking the 600 necklaces in Lauren's wagon. There were 50 necklaces in each long tube, so it took Noah a while to fit them all into the wagon.

Jack and Noah asked several friends to help sell the necklaces for $2 each, and they agreed to pay the friends $5 for every tube they emptied.

The sun was still shining brightly when the concert began at 6:00 that night. Jack and Noah knew that no one would buy the necklaces when it was sunny out, so they goofed around until the sun dropped below the trees.

At 8:30, Jack, Noah, Joey, Ryan and Aidan opened the first of twelve tubes. They each took three necklaces, cracked them along the edges until they glowed, and hung them around their necks. Each of them opened a new tube, listened to a few last words of advice from Noah, and then they all left in different directions.

As they headed off, Jack noticed that a few kids were already wearing glow-in-the-dark necklaces. That didn't surprise him, since a few families always brought their own. As he kept walking, however, he noticed more and more necklaces. He finally stopped and looked in every direction. Now that it was dark, he could tell that pretty much everyone in the park was already wearing a glow-in-the-dark necklace, including adults. In fact, most kids were wearing two or three.

A kid about Jack's age was standing nearby. "Hey," Jack said as he tapped the boy's shoulder, "can you tell me where you got those necklaces?"

The boy smiled. "There are like a hundred people all over the park, just giving them away. I've got ten of them in my backpack. Look at the writing," he said as held up one of his necklaces, "it's an advertisement for the company that pays for the concert. Can you believe these were all free? It's so cool!"

'Cool' was not exactly the word Jack was thinking. He tried to sell his necklaces for $2 each, but everyone wanted them for free. He wandered back to his parents at 9:30, and found Noah, Ryan, Joey and Aidan already there. Together, they had sold 10 necklaces, and they had wasted the 15 necklaces now hanging around their necks.

"We sold $20 worth?" asked Jack.

"Yep, that's it," replied Noah. "We have 575 necklaces left over…"

"…And barely $100 in cash left for our party."

At precisely 10:00, Jack and Noah laid down on the cool grass to watch the fireworks that were exploding directly above them. They had planned on having their heads cushioned by two pillowcases, filled to their limits with over one thousand dollars from the necklace sales. Instead, they were left wondering if the smoky haze settling over them was from the fireworks, or if it was all that was left of the coolest birthday party ever.

17 NO GIVING UP – SATURDAY, JULY 5

Jack usually slept in after a late night, but he woke at 6:00 a.m. and couldn't fall asleep again. He stomped down the staircase at 7:30 as soon as he heard his dad moving around in the kitchen.

"Hey, what did I say about no elephants in the house? Oh, it's just you, Jack. I could have sworn there was an elephant on the stairs," said his dad.

"THERE WILL BE NO ELEPHANTS," Jack heard his mom yell from the laundry room in the basement.

"Dad," Jack said, in a much quieter voice than his dad had just used, "what are the chances that Mom is going to change her mind about the elephant?"

"She's not yelling nearly as loud as she was last week. Give her another month, and she'll be a pushover. Anyway... how did your necklace sales go last night? Noah still seemed to have quite a few in his wagon at the end of the night."

"It didn't go so well, Dad."

"Well, that happens in business. How much money do you have for your party?"

"We started with $95, lost $3 at the first camp, lost $20 at the second camp, and made $309 at the third camp, so we were up to $381. But then we spent $15 on a peddler's license and $300 on the necklaces. Since we only sold $20 of necklaces, we're down to $86. Even worse, the store won't take back the necklaces we couldn't sell."

"But on the bright side, you've got enough necklaces to light up the city."

"Thanks, Dad, that makes me feel a lot better."

"Jack, you and Noah have been focused on making money the last four weeks, and all you've done is lose $9. Are you ready to call it quits and enjoy the rest of your summer?"

"There's six weeks until my birthday. We still have a chance to have the coolest birthday party ever. We'll just have to work a little harder to make it happen."

"I like your attitude, Jack. But remember – I've already given you my money for the party. If you lose the $86 you have left, then your party will consist of a cake, nine candles and no friends."

18 TESTING – MONDAY, JULY 7

Jack and Noah went back to work on Monday morning, putting slushie flyers on doorknobs around Noah's neighborhood. They also moved the slushie machine into Lauren's red wagon so they easily could move it from the house to the street.

Mrs. Patton made the first batch of slushies to be sure the boys had the right recipe. The boys thought it tasted good, but they each had three slushies and a whopper brain freeze before they were sure. They both had to go the bathroom a lot that day.

It cost $10 for the slushie mix to fill both tubs. They figured they could sell at least fifty slushies if they used small cups.

"This is going to be as easy as printing money," observed Jack.

"Yep, as easy as teaching a new dog old tricks," agreed Noah.

"Noah, I think you're supposed to say, 'as hard as teaching an old dog new tricks.'"

"How would I know? My parents won't let me have a dog."

19 COLD HARD CASH – WEDNESDAY, JULY 9

At nine o'clock on Wednesday morning, July 9, Noah and Jack began their career in the restaurant business. Dirk and Turk were dancing with their poster boards along Underwood Avenue. Lauren was in the front yard, doing her part by playing her 'Little Kids Sing Popular Songs' CD as loud as she could on a portable stereo. She also danced to the music, because she was certain that would attract people to their slushie stand.

Jack's dad had told the boys that half of all restaurants fail within one year of opening. In the first thirty minutes of their new business, they had no customers and not even one car had driven by the house.

Jack was certain that Dirk and Turk had deserted their posts on Underwood Avenue, so he walked up the street to spy on them. To his surprise, he found them still waving their poster boards as instructed, but Jack found one problem. The boys had switched signs by mistake.

"Dirk," Jack said, "your sign says 'Ice cold slushies, $2, turn right now.'"

"Yeah, I know. Every time I read it, I get thirstier."

"Dirk, when the cars go past you, what direction do they need to turn to get onto Noah's street?"

"That's easy, Jack. They need to turn left."

"But your sign says, 'turn right.' If they turn right, they're going to drive over a curb, cross over the sidewalk into Memorial Park, and pass over the pitcher's mound on the way to the playground."

"Whoa, Jack. Don't people know they can't drive on a baseball field?"

"Dirk, I think you have the wrong sign. Your sign should say 'turn left.' And since Turk is waving his sign at people coming in the opposite direction, his sign should say 'turn right.' Does that make sense?"

"Jack, I've never been that good with directions. So if you say I've got the wrong sign, then I believe you."

Once Jack convinced Turk to trade signs with Dirk, he returned to Noah's house. Mrs. Patton and baby Meredith were their first customers at 9:40. Jack suggested that Noah give them free slushies, but Noah made his mom pay. A car finally pulled up at 10:00, but she only wanted directions. Just before 11:00, an elderly woman from down the block stopped at the end of her walk, but she didn't have any money. She looked pretty thirsty, so Noah gave her a free slushie.

20 FREE SLUSHIE DAY – THURSDAY, JULY 10

Things didn't go much better on Thursday. Jack walked into Noah's garage just before 9:00.

"Hey, Noah, how's it going?"

"Perfecto. Today's the day our slushie stand goes big time."

"Uh, Noah, I'm not so sure about that."

"Come on, Jack, you've got to have a positive attitude."

"I do, Noah. But since you forgot to plug in the slushie machine this morning," he said, pointing at the silent machine, "I think we'll be serving cherry punch instead of cherry slushies."

Noah quickly plugged in the slushie machine, but the punch didn't turn into slushie until almost 10:00. It didn't matter, though. They didn't have one customer in the first hour. Jack walked a block to Underwood Avenue.

"Dirk, you're holding the wrong sign again."

"No way, Jack. You told me yesterday I was supposed to hold the 'turn left' sign. So that's what I'm doing."

"But yesterday you were standing over there," Jack said, pointing a block away to where Turk now stood, "and drivers going by you had to turn left to go to Noah's. But today you're here," and Jack pointed towards the ground, "and drivers going by you have to turn right to get to Noah's. Does that make sense?"

"Um, not so much."

"Dirk, if I told you to walk to Noah's house, how would you get there?"

"That's easy. I'd walk to the corner, turn right, and go straight for about one block."

"So now you understand why you should be holding the 'turn right' sign?"

"Not really."

"Dirk, please go switch signs with Turk."

"Whatever you say, Boss."

Jack walked back to the slushie stand and saw Noah waiting on the first customer of the day. It was Mrs. Churchill, the lady Noah had given a free slushie yesterday, and she brought along a friend from her Christian book club. Mrs. Patton and Lauren came again, but Mrs. Patton decided they could share a slushie. Four neighborhood kids arrived just before 11:00 looking for free slushies. Noah told them they didn't have to pay, but only because July 10th was National Free Slushie Day. Jack was annoyed at Noah, and told him so as soon as the four kids left with their drinks.

"Noah, why do you keep giving away slushies?"

"Jack, it's marketing. Advertising. I gave one away yesterday to that lady, and today she brought back a friend. I bet you those kids will come back tomorrow with money."

"But what if they don't?"

"Jack, National Free Slushie Day is only once a year. If they don't have money the next time they come back, then they're out of luck."

"I don't know, Noah. I don't like giving away anything for free. We need all the money we can get for our party."

📖 📖 📖 📖 📖 📖 📖 📖

The Taylor's nightly 'thanks to God' list always grew longer in the summer, when the kids weren't sitting in school all day.

"Watching Dad pick up Stella's poop, going to the bathroom, finding a squashed-up bug on the sidewalk…"

"Henry," interrupted Mrs. Taylor.

"Sorry, Mom. What I meant was going to the park, taking a family walk, playing kickball in the back yard with Dad, and… and finding a squashed-up bug on the sidewalk."

"How about you, Jack?"

"Family walk, kickball, seeing Noah, hot dogs for dinner, not having to pick up Stella's poop, not seeing a squashed-up bug on the sidewalk."

"Ugh," said Mr. Taylor. "How did we get stuck with two boys?"

"You got lucky," replied Jack.

"Yeah," said Henry, "you're definitely the luckiest parents in the entire world."

"And you're the luckiest kids in the world. Go to sleep."

21 THIRD TIME'S A CHARM? – FRIDAY, JULY 11

Friday started on a more promising note. Noah remembered to turn on the slushie machine as soon as he got out of bed, so the slushies were ready by the time Jack arrived. Even better, a car stopped right after Noah pulled the slushie wagon to the curb. Jack stayed in the garage to make sure the electrical cord stayed in the outlet, and then Lauren began showing Jack a dance move that she had learned from her favorite movie.

"Can I help you, Ma'am?" Noah asked, as a lady in a t-shirt, shorts and running shoes got out of the car.

"I'd love a slushie. I just finished a long run, and I could use something sweet."

"Great, one slushie coming right up."

Noah pulled down on the handle to fill a cup, but nothing came out. He let go of the handle and tried again. No slushie came out, but he could hear a grinding noise. Noah pulled the handle down a third time, and the slushie mix shot into the cup so quickly that most of it bounced out of the cup, landing on Noah's chest and face. He fell backward into the yard, mostly red and sticky from the waist up.

The handle was pushed down, so slushie continued to shoot out of the nozzle, along with bits of silver metal. The pieces of metal bounced off the wagon, and it sounded like whizzing bullets to Jack. When the shooting stopped, Jack and Lauren ran from the garage, but the left slushie tub was empty by the time they reached Noah. Well, almost empty.

"Noah," Jack asked, "why is there a fork in the tub? Or at least part of a fork in the tub?"

"Hey, that's where I left my fork," exclaimed Lauren. "I decided to help you guys by mixing the slushie after breakfast. I guess I must have dropped the fork."

"I….," said the lady, not quite what sure to do, but certain that she didn't want to drink a slushie that might have pieces of metal in it. "I'm…. I'm going to go now. Maybe I'll come back some other day." She hurried to her car and drove away.

Noah ran into the house to complain to Mrs. Patton about Lauren. Mrs. Patton ran out the front door, carrying Baby Meredith.

"Lauren, how could you ruin one of my new forks?"

"I was just trying to help Noah, Mom."

"Do you know how hard I'm going to have to work to get the slushie stain out of Noah's shirt?"

"Sorry?" Lauren wasn't sure why Mrs. Patton cared about Noah's shirt. Mrs. Patton always complained that Noah wore the same three shirts, and they all had stains on them already.

"Mom, Lauren ruined a sale, and one of the tubs emptied because of her. She totally should be grounded."

"Actually, Noah, you have to empty the other tub too. We've got to make sure there aren't any pieces of the fork in the other tub. Tell Dirk and Turk the stand is closed. You and Jack can clean out the tubs until Mrs. Taylor picks up Jack."

The boys had sold five slushies in a week and, after expenses, they had lost $23. Selling slushies was a lot harder than running a summer camp.

22 EXPLOSIVE IDEAS – TUESDAY, JULY 15

Jack and Noah had been so busy preparing for their slushie
stand that they didn't even go to their fourth summer camp on
Tuesday, July 8. Greta was in charge of everything that day, and
did a fine job keeping 94 kids under control. Crazy Luke behaved
for the second straight week, the fire trucks and ambulances
stayed away, and the boys earned a $327 profit.

The kids held their fifth camp on Tuesday, July 15, and over
one hundred children attended. Now that the camp was a month
old, Greta, Delaney and the rest of the camp counselors were
running out of ideas to keep the campers' attention. Fletch the
magician was running out of jokes – apparently there were only
so many ways to mess up a trick – and Stella had decided that
sleeping was far more important than chasing the two golden
retrievers during their tricks. Ralph's soccer ball tricks were even

getting boring, particularly since Crazy Luke was no longer throwing large rocks at Ralph's head.

Jack suggested that the counselors organize scavenger hunts. Mrs. Taylor told the counselors that they had to keep the kids within two blocks of the house, and they couldn't cross 52nd Street because it was too busy. In order to save money, Noah decided that instead of leaving stuff for the campers to find, the counselors should just make lists of things that could be found in the neighborhood.

Jacob and Rachel – the brother-and-sister team who now were the busiest babysitters in the city – took responsibility for making the scavenger hunt lists, primarily because they could spell better than everyone else. The list included things like collecting a four-leaf clover, a stick at least two feet long, and a smashed pop can. The campers also had to spot a rabbit and a cat, although not together, because everyone knows that rabbits and cats don't like each other.

The camp counselors agreed to only take two groups of kids on the scavenger hunts at one time. This allowed two counselors to be with each group. However, the main reason for taking small groups was that Mrs. Taylor didn't want the neighborhood to know that she had 100 kids in her backyard.

Jacob and Rachel were each in charge of a group of ten kids at about 10:30 that day. These were the last two groups going on a hunt, and they were also the youngest kids at camp. Jacob was in charge of the four-year-olds, including Crazy Luke, while Rachel's group consisted of ten very excited three-year-olds. The two groups ran into each other in front of a huge brick house – the Logan house – that was four houses down from the Taylor house. All of the previous groups had seen rabbits scooting away from a long row of bushes in front of the Logan house. Jacob was getting ready to scare a rabbit out of the bushes, but Crazy Luke beat him to it. Crazy Luke hadn't been particularly well behaved at today's camp, so when he darted from the group and began running circles in the Logan's front yard, Jacob wasn't too surprised. Jacob played junior high basketball and had legs twice as long as Crazy Luke's, so it didn't take him long to catch Luke by the back of his shirt.

"Hey, buddy," Jacob said as he let go of Luke's shirt, "did you forget the deal you made with Jack? If you behave today, Jack will give you $4 so you can buy firecrackers."

Crazy Luke laughed and said, "I don't need money. I have all kinds of firecrackers. I can go 'boom boom' all day long." And with that, he sprinted away, disappearing around the back of the Logan house.

The other three- and four-year-olds stopped looking for rabbits and started chanting, "Luke, Luke, Luke…" That wasn't a good sign, but Jacob and Rachel didn't know it. They hadn't been counselors at the first camp when Luke had climbed onto the Taylor roof.

Jacob walked back to the sidewalk and looked at his sister Rachel, who simply shrugged. She didn't have any better luck controlling Crazy Luke, so she wasn't about to help. While Jacob was still pondering whether to search for Crazy Luke in the Logan's backyard, Crazy Luke skipped down the Logan driveway, flew past Jacob and Rachel with a big grin on his face, and headed towards the Taylor house four doors away.

Jacob started to chase after Crazy Luke. However, the explosion stopped him cold in his tracks.

Jacob had watched some cool explosions on TV and in movies, but he'd never seen one in person. So for that reason alone, most people would be willing to forgive Jacob for screaming at the top of his lungs. In a span of ten seconds, at the Logan house with the bushes and the rabbits in the big yard where they were now standing, everything went a little crazy.

The first explosion broke all of the Logan's windows. Glass flew out of the house like icicles before lodging in the grass or shattering on the driveway. Then the front door blew open, fell off its hinges, and dropped onto the porch floor. The burglar alarm in the house began wailing but stopped a few seconds later after a third explosion shook the house and echoed off surrounding homes. A fourth explosion sent a small television set, two chairs and half of a piano flying out of what had been the living room window. Finally, a puff of flames and smoke shot out of the chimney top, and then fire started crackling throughout the house.

Rachel had to punch Jacob in the arm to get his attention. They ran back to the Taylor house as fast as they could, with two other counselors and nineteen little kids right on their heels.

📖 📖 📖 📖 📖 📖 📖 📖

The four explosions and the burning house had been noticed by, oh, a few neighbors and half of the Omaha fire department. Fire truck sirens could be heard within two minutes, and 52nd Street was soon lined with pumper trucks, ambulances and curious spectators.

Police cars came, too. Despite everything going on, a few neighbors had remembered that a group of about twenty kids had run out of the Logan's front yard right after the explosions. Mrs. Taylor was not surprised when the police knocked at her front door. She tried to appear calm, which was almost impossible given what had just happened.

The police captain looked serious, as did the six other policemen standing behind him. At least they didn't have their guns drawn. "Good morning, Ma'am. We have a report that a large group of children were near the house down the street when it exploded. Several neighbors indicated that the group of children ran up your driveway."

Just then a very loud rendition of Mike Douglas' latest camp song began in the backyard. The song, "I Eat Pickles for Breakfast," was a huge hit with the campers. Mrs. Taylor smiled as if she hadn't heard a thing.

The police captain looked even more grumpy now. "Can you explain what is going on here?"

It took quite of bit of explaining, actually, and 11:00 was quickly approaching. The police had blocked off the street, so the moms and their mini-vans could not reach the Taylor house. Policemen can be pushy, but moms can be downright rude when they're in a hurry.

Mrs. Taylor quickly found Jacob and Rachel, and they were taken to separate bedrooms upstairs for questioning. The other two counselors and twenty kids that had seen the explosion were sent to the basement. They had been easy to find, because every one of them except Crazy Luke had a layer of black dust on their clothes and faces. Crazy Luke was almost able to escape questioning, but one of the three-year-old kids ratted him out in exchange for a candy bar from a policeman.

The police allowed the rest of the campers and counselors to leave shortly after 11:00. The mothers of the twenty children stuck in the basement waited in the backyard for their children to be released. They probably would have stayed anyway, because there weren't too many things more exciting than waiting for a bunch of young criminals to be escorted out of the house in handcuffs.

By noon, the fire was under control, although it was clear that the Logan house was ruined. Mr. Taylor had come home for lunch, and he brought along Mr. Dooley, a lawyer friend, just in case the police got really mad. Two moms who were waiting for their four-year-olds to be released started a lunch of hot dogs and chicken chunks.

At 12:30, the fire marshal left the fire and came to the Taylor's. For whatever reason – maybe because there were a bunch of criminals in the Taylor house – the police department had decided to establish their command post in the Taylor's front yard. The fire marshal and the police captain huddled together for a few minutes, and then they came into the house. Mr. Taylor met them at the door. Jack and Noah were sitting in the dining room, having been ordered to do so by Mrs. Taylor. If Jack and Noah were going to be arrested, Mrs. Taylor didn't want the policemen walking upstairs to Jack's bedroom with their dirty shoes.

"Mr. Taylor, it appears that the explosion was caused by a gas leak in the Logan's house."

"That's too bad, but at least the children did nothing to cause the explosion…"

"Actually," the police captain said, "they did cause the explosion. It appears that a four-year-old male," and he paused to look down at his small notebook, "who goes by the name of Crazy Luke lit some firecrackers on the Logan's back porch. The sparks from the firecrackers created the explosion. I need to talk to whomever was in charge of Crazy Luke at the time of the explosion."

Jack and Noah's eyes bulged. Goodbye coolest party ever, hello prison.

23 THE INTERROGATION – TUESDAY, JULY 15

Jack, Noah, Luke, Jacob and Rachel were gathered around the dining room table. The police captain took off his fancy hat and sat in Mr. Taylor's regular chair at the head of the table. Jack called his dad's spot the 'Chair of Authority,' and the police captain looked pretty comfortable in it. Mr. Taylor and Mr. Dooley stood behind Jack, while Greta and Henry secretly listened from the kitchen. Noah pulled a turkey sandwich out of his baseball cap. Jack shook his head.

"How can you be this skinny when you eat all the time?" Jack asked.

"Mom says I have a high pessimism," said Noah. "That means I burn a lot of celeries."

"Let's get this started," said the police captain in a very serious voice.

"Do I need a lawyer?" asked Jack.

"What's a lawyer?" asked Noah.

"When you get in trouble," Jack said, "you hire a lawyer to get you out of trouble. They wear suits and use really big words, and they talk to judges all the time. Some lawyers spend all day chasing ambulances, but Mr. Dooley here doesn't do that. Dad says he just sits at his desk and plays computer games."

Mr. Dooley turned to look at Mr. Taylor. Mr. Taylor gave one of those smiles that parents make when their kids have said something embarrassing.

"Why do you think you need a lawyer?" replied the police captain, trying to ignore Mr. Dooley.

"On TV, that's the first thing someone says when they're about to be questioned by the police. Plus," he said, looking out the window, "there are at least ten policemen in our front yard, and I heard that policemen get a bonus for every little kid they arrest."

"Who told you that?"

"My dad."

"When did he tell you that?"

"Whenever me and my brother and sister are fighting or being bad. He says that policeman love to arrest kids who are being bad because they get a bonus. Right, Dad?"

"Sure, Jack, but let's not worry about that now. Captain, this is Mr. Dooley," Mr. Taylor said, introducing his attorney friend, "and he is here in a semi-official manner to represent our family."

"Is he going to charge me for this? I don't want this coming out of my birthday money!" This was the most upset Jack had been all day.

"If I do represent you," said Mr. Dooley, "I'll probably have to charge you something."

"Forget it then," said Jack. "Greta," he yelled, "where are you?"

"Right here, Jack," replied Greta, stepping out of the kitchen. "Do you need me to do some legal research for you?"

"Just stay nearby, Greta. I may need your help."

"OK, then," said the police captain, "let's get back to work. Luke," he said, turning to look at Crazy Luke, "is it true you lit some firecrackers behind the Logan house?"

Luke looked like he was getting ready to cry. He slowly nodded his head.

"And where did you get those firecrackers?"

Luke slowly lifted his right arm, straightened it out, and pointed it directly at Jack.

"THAT'S NOT TRUE, THAT'S NOT TRUE," howled Jack, certain that he was now going to jail. "I gave Crazy Luke eight dollars because he behaved, but I didn't buy him any firecrackers."

"Why would you pay a neighbor kid to behave?" The police captain had kids of his own, but he'd never heard this kind of story.

"We have this summer camp every Tuesday," Jack started, knowing that this would certainly lead to more questions, "and Luke kept doing things that caused us to call the fire department for help. So I figured if I paid him to behave during camp, we wouldn't have to call the fire department again."

"That plan worked real well," Mr. Taylor whispered under his breath to Mr. Dooley. "There are over one hundred firemen here today."

"Oh, that makes sense," said the fire marshal, who had been standing behind the police captain, "no wonder our drivers knew where to go. I hear your mom makes great lemonade."

"Luke," the police captain said, trying to get control of the interrogation, "who bought the firecrackers for you?"

Luke shook his head. "I'll never tell!"

The police captain stared at Luke. Luke crossed his arms and stared back. Crazy Luke was not going to be intimidated by the captain. The captain stood up and took out his handcuffs.

"Daddy," screamed Luke. "Daddy bought them! Daddy buys them whenever I want them. He tells me to go 'boom' all day long! I give up! Don't take me to prison!"

"OK, he confessed, you can go now," said Jack hurriedly, standing up and hoping that he was no longer in trouble.

"Sit down, Jack," said the police captain sternly, pointing Jack back into his chair. "You didn't buy the firecrackers, but since it's your camp, you were still in charge of Crazy Luke, right? You and Noah were the ones who should have stopped him from blowing up a house."

"Does it matter that we didn't want to be in charge of him?" asked Noah.

"How were we supposed to know that a little kid could blow up a house?" Jack added. "He's the worst kid on our block, but he's never blown up a house before."

"Are we sure about that?" asked Mr. Taylor, to no one in particular.

"Mr. Captain, sir," said Greta, tired of hearing the boys begging for mercy, "even if Jack and Noah were responsible for Crazy Luke, I don't see how that matters."

The police captain shook his head. With all the adults in the room, he was now going to have to argue with a little girl. "What do you mean, young lady?"

"Well, I've done a little Internet research on natural gas explosions. If Luke started the explosion by lighting firecrackers outside the house, that probably means that the house was so full of gas that it was leaking outside…"

"That's true," said the fire marshal.

"And the Internet says that if a house is filled with natural gas, then practically anything can start the explosion. A candle, one of the appliances, even the pressure of all the gas inside the house. In fact, the Internet says that when an explosion like this is started from the outside, it probably would have started on its own at some point – possibly even when the Logans came home and opened their back door."

"That's also true," said the fire marshal.

"So," Greta continued, "because Crazy Luke lit those firecrackers, isn't it possible that he might have saved the lives of Mr. and Mrs. Logan?"

"Well….I don't know about that," stammered the fire marshal.

"And if the gas had continued to leak until tonight, isn't it possible that the explosion would have been even larger – maybe so big that it destroyed other houses besides the Logan's? And at night, more people would have been home from work, so Luke might have also saved the lives of the people who live next to the Logan house?"

Crazy Luke sat up in his chair and puffed out his chest. "I'm a hero!"

"Well…I don't know… about that either," stuttered the fire marshal.

"What do you mean, you don't know?" demanded the police captain. "Aren't you supposed to know everything about fires?"

"I suppose it's possible. I mean, Greta makes some good points, but… well, she makes some good points. She's right. If Luke hadn't caused the explosion in the morning, then it would have been much worse if it happened later in the day. Instead of just the Logan house, the explosion would have destroyed at least two more houses."

Crazy Luke stood up and flexed his muscles. He had saved two houses.

"But," Greta said, "Crazy Luke still violated three city laws. Four-year-olds aren't supposed to have firecrackers. Firecrackers can only be lit the two weeks before July 4th. And," she paused, before making an educated guess, "he has worn the same pair of underwear three days in a row. I think he still has to go to jail."

Luke knew he had been busted. He put his head down on the table. Greta winked at the police captain, who cleared his throat.

"I agree, Greta. However, Luke," and at this, Crazy Luke raised his head just enough for his eyes to show, "if you promise to stay out of trouble until you're ten, and if you change your underwear every day, then you don't have to go to prison today. But if I hear you're causing trouble, then I've got a pair of kid-sized handcuffs just for you. Do you understand?"

Luke nodded weakly. He looked like he was going to throw up. Greta got a mixing bowl from the kitchen and put it in front of Luke.

Jack spoke up. "So are we still in trouble for not watching Luke? Do we have to pay for a new house?" Jack was pretty sure they wouldn't have enough money to buy a new house and still have the coolest birthday party ever.

"No, you don't have to pay for a new house," the police captain replied. "I'm sure the Logans have insurance for that. However..."

"This is when he tells us that we have to go to jail," Noah whispered to Jack.

The police captain continued, "we are a little concerned about the hundred or so children who were in your backyard at the time of the explosion. I honestly don't know what rules you're breaking, but it seems like there ought to be at least a few."

"Don't worry, Jack," said Henry, who had come out of his hiding place, "I'll visit you in prison."

24 PUBLICITY –TUESDAY, JULY 15

The exploding house and police investigation were the top stories on all the television news shows on Tuesday night and in the newspaper on Wednesday morning. In fact, the newspaper assigned three reporters to the explosion, and they were working hard to find stories.

The newspaper ran an article on the explosion, the near-death experiences of twenty-four children ('near-death' sounded more interesting than 'their faces got dirty') and the fire department's quick response. One of the reporters discovered that ambulances are stocked with clean pairs of underwear for occasions like this, and the service was needed by quite a few of the three- and four-year-olds who saw the explosion. (If they were like Luke, they'd be wearing their new pair for the next week.) It was also reported that several mothers needed special counseling because of the explosion. That wasn't quite true; Mrs. Taylor told Jack that the 'counseling session' was an excuse for the moms to have a nice dinner without kids.

The newspaper contacted over a dozen campers and moms who said that the camp was the best thing the kids had done all summer. The kids said things like, "It was fun even before they blew up the house," and "my counselor lets me draw on his face with a marker." The moms said things like, "my house is quiet for two hours every Tuesday," and "I sure wish they'd hold camp every day."

The Logans were interviewed on what remained of their front lawn. They thanked the fire department, and they thanked their neighbors for giving them clothes and a place to sleep that night. They also told the reporters they were thankful that Crazy Luke had saved their lives. Finally, they said they were moving. There were far too many fire trucks and ambulances on their street for their liking.

One of the television stations filmed the bomb squad unit from the police department when it arrived at Crazy Luke's house a few hours after the interrogation. After they searched the house for two hours, they left with four boxes of firecrackers – each box was the size of a large toy chest – and two four-foot rockets that Luke had apparently built himself.

One newspaper reporter focused on Jack and Noah's summer camp and whether it was illegal. The chief of police told the reporter that the summer camp did indeed violate several laws, and he would be visiting the Taylor house at 5:00 p.m. that day to issue all sorts of tickets. Greta met the chief of police at the front door when he arrived.

"I need to speak with Jack Taylor and his parents, please."

"Hello, Mr. Chief Person. I'm Greta. The newspaper reporter called to tell me you are going to take Jack to jail. Before you do that, I thought you should know that Jack is following the rules."

"Young lady, I'm not taking Jack to jail. I'm simply going to…"

Greta interrupted him. "Mr. Chief Person, it doesn't matter where you're taking him. He's not breaking the rules. Here," she said, handing him several pieces of paper, "are the rules of the State of Nebraska for day care providers, preschools, and sports and activities camps. As you'll see under Section 14.2, paragraph (a), the rules for a sports and activities camp are fairly simple, and Jack appears to be following all of them."

The chief of police spent a minute reviewing the information. "Where did you find these rules?"

"They're on the Internet, Mr. Sir Chief Person. Don't you ever use a computer?" The chief of police shook his head. "Anyway, my client is prepared…"

"Who is your client?"

"Jack Taylor, of course. I represent him. As I was saying, my client is prepared to do more than what the law requires. He plans to add a portable bathroom in the backyard, and he will now have two adult supervisors at every camp. Both supervisors are moms, so they know pretty much everything there is to know about kids."

Jack had agreed to add the extra bathroom; he thought it would be a good chance for him to do some serious thinking outside. Plus, it's just a lot more fun to go to the bathroom outside. As for the adult supervisors, Greta was guessing that Mrs. Patton and Mrs. Taylor would be at the rest of the camps. The whole exploding house deal had made Mrs. Taylor nervous.

The chief of police stood at the door, not quite sure what to do.

"And one more thing, Mr. Chief Dude. The police website says that you have a four-year-old girl and a six-year-old boy. We have room for them next week at camp. Just be sure to call early if you want to guarantee their spots."

Greta closed the front door, leaving the chief of police standing alone on the Taylor's porch. Mrs. Taylor called to Greta from the kitchen.

"Greta, was someone at the front door?"

"It was just a salesman, Mom," said Greta. "Absolutely nothing to worry about."

During one of Jack and Noah's final interviews on the day of the explosion, the newspaper reporter asked if he could follow up with Jack the following day.

"Well, I'm a little busy tomorrow. I get up at 8:00, have to eat breakfast, be at our slushie stand from 9:00 until 11:00, eat lunch, go swimming, practice piano, eat dinner… maybe you could call around 6:00 p.m.?"

"What's a slushie stand?"

"A stand that sells slushies. At Noah's house. Slushies are the best drink in the world on a hot summer day. You should come get one."

"You run a summer camp and a slushie stand?"

"We sell glow-in-the-dark necklaces, too," piped in Noah. "Do you want to buy 575 of them?"

"Why do you have a slushie stand?" asked the reporter.

"Because we have a slushie machine," replied Jack. "Why keep the best drink in the world to ourselves?"

"Do you charge people for these slushies?"

"Of course we do. We're businessmen."

"You're eight."

"Yep, we're eight-year-old businessmen."

"Who happen to run a summer camp and a slushie stand," the reporter said, as if he didn't believe it.

"Don't forget the glow-in-the-dark necklaces," added Noah. "We're giving discounts if you buy at least ten of them."

The reporter ignored Noah and turned back to Jack. "You must be making a lot of money doing this."

"Not much so far. But we made over $300 today with our camp. And I've got a real good feeling about the slushie stand at Noah's house."

"Why's that?"

"Dude, haven't you been listening? It's the best drink in the world on a hot summer day. And we've got a lot of hot summer days coming up."

"So what are you going to do with all of this money?"

"I turn nine on August 18. We're throwing a big party for my friends and my sister and my sister's friends, but that's it. No other girls, no little kids."

"How big is this party?"

"Super big. Elephant rides..."

"THERE WILL BE NO ELEPHANTS!" Jack's mom was listening to the interview through the kitchen window.

Jack leaned in and talked more quietly. "Elephant rides, non-scary clowns, bazooka target practice, octopus wrestling, everything you could ever think of that is cool."

"Can I come?"

"If you write about the slushie stand in the newspaper, you can have the first elephant ride."

"THERE WILL BE NO ELEPHANTS!" Jack's mom sure could hear well.

Jack winked at the reporter and whispered, "Trust me. There will be plenty of elephants."

25 WORKING FOR A LIVING – WEDNESDAY, JULY 16

Noah's Slushie Stand returned for its second week of business on Wednesday, the same day the newspaper had several articles about Jack and Noah. Dirk and Turk were still interested in holding the signs, especially since Jack and Noah were now famous. Noah promised Dirk and Turk an extra hour on his video game for each day they sold at least forty slushies. That was apparently why the brothers decided to begin dressing up. Today they were dressed as a gorilla and Spiderman. They were also holding the correct signs.

Nearly everyone in Omaha read the local newspaper, and it soon became clear that business at the slushie stand was going to improve. Cars began stopping as soon as Jack pulled the slushie wagon to the curb at 9:00. Six ladies in a walking club arrived at 9:15, and ten women from the Christian book club were close behind them. Pretty soon it seemed like everyone in the neighborhood had come to the slushie stand. Lauren gave up her dance routine to help collect money (which was hard, because she hadn't learned how to count yet and, more importantly, she was born to dance), and Mrs. Patton began serving slushies as soon as baby Meredith went down for her morning nap.

Noah recognized Mrs. Churchill. "Thanks for coming back, Mrs. Churchill, and thanks for bringing all your friends."

"You're quite welcome, Noah. Here, I cut your picture out of the paper," and she handed him the newspaper clipping. "You know, I've always wanted to ride an elephant."

"Uh, Mrs. Churchill, our party is only for eight- and nine-year-old boys."

"Noah, unless you want a Christian book club protest on your hands, you might want to think over who is on your invitation list." Mrs. Churchill smiled, not exactly a friendly smile, and walked away. Noah couldn't decide if she was serious.

Jack had to refill the first tub by 9:45, and the new mixture was barely frozen by the time the second tub emptied at 10:30. Jack's mom arrived to take him home, but she had to wait in the driveway until 11:20 so the boys could serve all the customers standing in line. By then both tubs were dry, and several disappointed customers promised to come back the following day.

Jack and Noah met at the swimming pool later that afternoon. "Jack," Noah said, "our slushie stand is a huge hit!"

"Totally. Why didn't we think of blowing up a house before this week?"

"Jack!"

"Sorry, Mom. Just joking. We didn't plan to blow up that house."

"I sure hope so. By the way, I have a present for you at home," Mrs. Taylor said. Jack knew immediately what it was.

"What color this month, Mom?"

"They're plaid – a combination of bright green and bright purple. I'm sure you'll have the nicest pants in church on Sunday."

📖 📖 📖 📖 📖 📖 📖 📖

Later that night, Noah and his mom began making extra slushies and storing them in buckets in the freezer so they could quickly refill the tubs as they became empty. On Thursday, Noah and Jack were so busy between 9:00 and 11:00 that they didn't have time to drink their own slushies.

However, Friday started off a little slow. Mrs. Patton had insisted that they try a mango slushie in one tub and an asparagus slushie in the other tub. Noah tried his best to sell them.

"On sale now, Omaha's first-ever mango slushie, with a special mix created from mangos that were freshly squeezed sometime in the last three years!" There was a line of people waiting for slushies, but no one moved forward.

"Step right up for the world-famous asparagus slushie, created from a secret Patton family recipe." No one stepped up.

"My mom says this is the healthiest slushie in the world, made with asparagus and lettuce straight from our garden. This slushie has never been shared with the world before today…" and within ten minutes, it was pretty clear it would never be shared again. Jack and Noah dumped the mango and asparagus slushies on some weeds Mr. Patton wanted killed, and cherry and strawberry slushies were being served by 9:20.

Their sales ledger for the second week was pretty impressive:

	Cups Sold
Wed, July 16	110
Thurs, July 17	123
Fri, July 18	83

During the second week of the slushie stand, they made almost $600 after expenses. It was good money, but the slushie stand was taking up most of their time together. After the slushie stand closed on Friday, Noah wondered if a change was needed.

"Making money is one thing," he told Jack as they cleaned out the slushie machine in his garage, "but holding down a steady job is getting boring."

"No kidding," replied Jack. "How do adults do this every day?"

"My dad said he doesn't do any work, he just tells people what to do all day."

"He gets paid to do that?" Jack couldn't believe a job could be that easy.

"Oh, yeah, loads of money. He told me he has to get a box to carry home all the money he makes every week. He showed me the box once. It's huge!"

"So maybe we should just tell people what to do from now on."

"Definitely. Let's have Dirk and Turk start selling slushies," Noah said. "Dirk told me his mom just lost her job, so I think we should pay them more. How about each of them get $5 and two hours of video game playing per day?"

"Maybe we should throw in two free slushies per day, too, and give them official name badges. That might get us one of those 'Best Bosses of the Year' awards."

"That would definitely do it. OK, I'll tell Dirk and Turk to find two friends to hold the poster boards. If they don't like video games, we'll pay them $5 each."

"Noah, if we have four people working for us at the slushie stand, we're going to make a lot of money."

"How much, do you think?"

"I'd guess at least $1 million. Maybe more. You had better get some boxes from your dad to carry all of our money."

"Wow, $1 million. Do you think that's too much to spend on a birthday party?"

"You can't ever have enough money for a birthday party, Noah. But $1 million is a good start. Maybe we can just buy an elephant instead of renting one."

26 PLANNING, PART 2 – MONDAY, JULY 21

On Monday, July 21, Jack and Noah began to worry. Jack's birthday was only four weeks away, and they didn't have one thing planned. The first thing they did on Monday morning was to count up all the money they had earned so far:

Parent money	$45
Allowance money	50
Camp June 17	(3)
Camp June 24	(20)
Camp July 1	309
Necklace sales, July 4	(295)
Camp July 8	327
Slushie stand, July 9-11	(23)
Camp July 15	358
Slushie stand July 16-18	587
Total	$1,335

"Noah, I'm not sure if we're going to get to $1 million." Jack had been thinking all weekend about what it would be like to be a millionaire, but if his math was right, they needed to earn $998,665 in the next four weeks to reach it.

"That's OK, Jack," Noah said as he spied half of a Pop-Tart underneath a pillow. "It's amazing how long these things stay fresh... anyway, two weeks ago we only had $86, so $1,335 is a pretty big improvement. Plus, I think we'll make about $1,400 per week between the camp and the slushie stand, so we should earn at least $5,600 in the next four weeks. That will give us $7,000 to spend on the party."

"It's not $1 million, but that still has to be enough to buy an elephant."

"YOU ARE NOT GOING TO BUY AN ELEPHANT!"

"How can your mom hear us in the attic? I thought she was outside."

"I swear, Noah, she can read my mind. Every time I think about doing something bad, she catches me before I do it."

"Jack, are you really going to spend $7,000 on your birthday party?" Greta had been lying on the attic couch, but the boys hadn't noticed her. "I mean, your party cost $40 last year, and now you want to spend $7,000? Mom and Dad keep telling us about all the people who have lost their jobs, and we see all the poor people when we volunteer at the soup kitchen. Don't you think you ought to do something good with some of that money?"

"Greta, when you have a chance to buy an elephant, do you think you're going to want to give your money away?"

"You can't buy an elephant for $7,000, and even if you could, we don't have any room for it. You've got to stop thinking like a boy." With that, Greta stomped down the stairs.

"What do you think about all that?" asked Noah.

"I think we need a lock for the attic door," replied Jack. "We can't have people walking into our office whenever they feel like it."

"What does she mean, 'stop thinking like a boy'? How do girls think?"

"FOR ONE THING, GIRLS DON'T DO THEIR THINKING IN THE BATHROOM!" Greta's hearing was as good as Mrs. Taylor's.

The boys quickly forgot Greta's comments and dove back into party planning. Jack asked his mom to call her friend at the zoo again, but she refused to help Jack with anything that had to do with an elephant. Jack called the zoo phone number and eventually was connected to Duncan, his mom's friend.

"Mr. Duncan, Sir, this is Jack Taylor. My mom called you last month about renting an elephant. Have you found anyone who would rent one?"

"No, Jack. Zoos just don't rent out elephants," replied Duncan.

"OK, I'm prepared to buy one of yours. I can pay about $7,000."

"Jack, that's a lot of money, but elephants cost more than $100,000. Plus, they eat at least one hundred pounds of food per day and need a lot of medical attention, so they are very expensive to own. On top of that, they poop quite a bit. I've been in your backyard before, and I'm afraid your entire backyard would be covered in elephant dung by the end of the first day."

"Dung?" Jack had never heard that word.

"Sorry, Jack. Dung is a polite word for animal poop."

"Does dung smell?" Jack loved learning new words, especially fun words like this.

"Oh, quite a bit," replied Duncan.

"Even worse than Stella's dung?"

"Much, much worse."

"OK, forget it. Thanks for your time, Mr. Duncan."

With an elephant out of the question for the moment, the boys turned to clowns. Noah called the Amazing Arthur, the semi-crazy magician who knew a lot of clowns.

"Mr. Amazing, this is Noah Patton. Mr. Taylor spoke to you last month about how much a non-scary clown would cost for a birthday party. Did you happen to read the newspaper article about our summer camp?"

"I have," replied Arthur.

"Well, Mr. Amazing, I have a business proposal for you. I want you and four non-scary clowns to come to Jack's party. I'll pay you $500. I also want you to do magic tricks at our camp for the next four weeks for free."

"For free? You've got to be kidding!" Arthur exclaimed.

Noah paused for a moment. "Actually, sir, I'm not. You see, we've been getting phone calls all weekend, and it looks like we're going to have over 200 kids at tomorrow's camp. Reporters from two TV stations and the newspaper are coming. If the campers think you're funny, I bet a bunch of moms would hire you for birthday parties."

Arthur didn't sound completely convinced. "OK, I'll agree to work at your camp tomorrow, but I won't promise anything beyond that."

Noah hung up and flashed a big smile at Jack. The boys had, in fact, been taking calls all weekend from mothers who wanted to reserve a spot at camp. It probably helped that Greta had sent an e-mail last Thursday warning mothers that the camp might be 'sold out.' Mothers could reserve their children's spots at camp for an extra $2. By the time Noah had spoken with Arthur, 180 reservations had been taken at $6 each. That worked out to more than $1,000.

Mrs. Taylor had been willing to put up with 100 kids, but she decided that 200 might destroy her house. To make matters worse, the boys couldn't find any more backyards to rent. Mrs. Taylor called the courthouse and arranged to rent a huge covered pavilion at Elmwood Park for $50 per hour. Greta sent out another e-mail notifying moms that the camp location had changed. The boys asked the newspaper to print the new location in Tuesday's paper, but the editor refused. Jack figured he didn't like kids.

As the reservation list kept growing, Jack made a panicked phone call to Rachel to find more counselors.

"Rachel, we have over 200 reservations for tomorrow's camp. Can you find some more volunteer counselors?"

"Holy cow, Jack, how many do you want?"

"Probably only twenty more." Noah had thought that ten would be enough, but Jack liked the idea of having more people to supervise. He kept thinking about Mr. Patton's boxes of money.

"Twenty? Are you crazy, Jack? You want me to find twenty more counselors to work for free?"

Jack didn't know what to say. He didn't think he could afford to pay them, but he definitely needed more counselors. Noah watched while Jack stammered and stuttered. Finally, he took the phone away from Jack.

"Rachel, this is Noah. Here's the deal. If you can find us twenty more counselors, Jack and I will help your Girl Scout troop sell cookies next January. We already have the biggest summer camp in the city, and I'm pretty sure we could help you sell the most cookies in the city next year."

Rachel paused for a moment, but Noah knew she'd say 'yes.' Everyone at school knew that in each of the past three years Rachel's Girl Scout troop had finished second in Omaha in cookie sales, and Rachel really wanted to win next year.

"Fine, I'll find twenty counselors. But I want a ride on the elephant."

"Sure, you can have a ride on the elephant. Thanks, Rachel." Noah hung up.

"Noah, why did you promise her a ride on the elephant? We just found out that there won't be an elephant."

"No, Jack," Noah replied. "We just found out that we couldn't buy an elephant. There's still a chance that we can get an elephant without buying it. You have to believe, Jack."

The boys crossed a few other items off the activity list for the birthday party. By 11:00, they had also arranged to have a super huge bounce house ($250) and two face painters ($200) at the birthday party. Including the money for the clowns and the Elmwood Park pavilion, they had spent $1,050 of their money in one day, and suddenly August 18 didn't seem that far away.

"Noah, have you ever spent $1,000 in one day?"

"I haven't even seen $1,000 before this week. The most expensive thing I've ever bought was a video game."

"My dad always said that the most expensive thing he ever bought was a box of 10,000 diapers."

"I bet that was a big box. My mom only buys 60 diapers at a time."

"Noah, they weren't all in one box. But think about how many diapers Meredith uses in one day? At least five?"

"Maybe ten."

"If Dirk and Turk's mom has lost her job, how is she going to pay for their little sister's diapers?

"I have no idea."

27 THE HARD QUESTION – TUESDAY, JULY 22

The next day started early. The sun was already too bright at 8:00, warning everyone that it was going to be a hot, dry day. Jack and Noah usually stayed in bed until 8:00 on summer mornings, but they had to get up at 7:00 today to start preparing for camp. Mrs. Taylor and Mrs. Patton loaded up their minivans with coolers of lemonade and boxes of snacks. At 7:30, they met with Jacob, Rachel, Greta and Delaney at Jack's house to review the camp schedule and counselor assignments.

At 8:30, all the neighbor kids jumped into the vans for the short drive to the park. Mrs. Taylor gasped as she turned the corner into the park; there were cars and kids everywhere. Two policemen were directing traffic, and television reporters were already filming kids running around the park.

Although the increased number of campers could have been a disaster, Jack and Noah's gang organized the camp with precision.

Greta, Noah, Jack and Mrs. Patton were in charge of registration, and campers were given different colored nametags to identify which counselors they had. Jacob and Rachel directed the campers to the counselors, and by 9:15 the camp activities were underway. The Amazing Arthur was almost late for his 10:00 show because he had to park three blocks away.

Noah and Jack had decided that it wasn't fair to charge $6 to the campers with reservations and only $4 to campers without reservations, so the price for all campers was raised to $6. The extra twenty Girl Scouts came in handy because 324 kids registered for camp. After expenses, the camp profit that day was $1,723.

Once Arthur started performing, the television reporters asked Jack and Noah for an interview. After asking several questions about how they organized such a big event, they asked a really hard one.

"Are you really going to spend all your money on a birthday party? Some people might say that it's selfish to spend so much money for one party."

"I don't think it's selfish at all," replied Jack. "It's not even close to being selfish. Noah and I have worked hard all summer to earn money for this birthday party. I only turn nine once, and that's a big day in my life. It's my birthday and I can do whatever I want with the money." With that, he turned away from the camera and went back to the pavilion to re-count the camp money.

At 5:00 that night, the Taylor family huddled around the TV so they could watch the news story about the summer camp. Unfortunately, almost the entire story focused on how much the boys were going to spend on Jack's birthday party. Mr. and Mrs. Taylor were more than a little mad when the story was finished.

"Jack, you need to stay away from TV cameras. You are officially the most spoiled kid in Omaha, or at least people will think so after they watch the news. How much money do you have?"

"We made $1,723 today, so now we've got about $2,900. We should have at least $7,000 by my birthday."

"So I'll ask the same question as the reporter," said Mr. Taylor, who was really looking annoyed. "Do you think it's right to spend $7,000 on a birthday party for a nine-year-old?"

"Dad, you and Mom and the Pattons made a deal with us. You agreed that we could spend whatever we made this summer on the party. Are you breaking our agreement?"

Mrs. Taylor tried a softer approach. "Jack, we didn't think you would even make $10 the entire summer. What you've done is nothing short of incredible. However, because you've been so successful, you simply can't spend all this money on your party.

Even if you invited everyone in your grade at school – what's that, sixty kids - you're still going to be spending almost $100 per kid."

"Mom, there's no way I'm inviting any of the girls in my grade, so it would only be thirty kids. Anyway, a deal is a deal. It's our money, and we're going to spend it however we like."

Jack left the living room, and went straight to the attic bathroom. He needed some serious thinking time. He couldn't believe his bad luck. He and Noah had become the most successful 8-year-old businessmen in the history of Omaha, and now everyone was trying to make them feel bad about spending their profits. The rules had been changed, and it didn't seem fair.

📖 📖 📖 📖 📖 📖 📖 📖

At 6:00, the Pattons and Taylors met for dinner at Mama's Pizza, a local pizza joint with good video games. Mama's Pizza wasn't exactly in the best part of town, so the Taylors passed a bunch of run-down houses and a homeless shelter on the way there. Jack watched the people standing in the shade in the front of their houses, trying to find a way to cool off since they couldn't afford air conditioning. He saw little kids, dressed in dirty clothes, playing tag and jumping rope in front of the shelter. He wondered if any of those people had lost their jobs, like Dirk and Turk's mom.

Outside the front door of Mama's Pizza, Mr. Taylor stopped to talk to a man holding a paper cup. Mr. Taylor called Jack over.

"Jack, this is Mr. Cousins. Do you remember him?"

"I think so," he said, turning to Mr. Cousins. "Don't you work at the grocery store? I think you put my mom's groceries into bags and carry them out to the car for her."

"Well, Jack, I used to do that," said Mr. Cousins. He sounded tired. "But the grocery store decided that the people who run the cash registers could also bag the groceries, so they didn't need me anymore. I was just telling your dad that I've been out of work for two months."

"I'm sorry to hear that, Mr. Cousins. I hope you find a job real soon."

"Thanks, Jack, and thank you, Mr. Taylor." He and Mr. Taylor shook hands.

After the Pattons and Taylors had ordered their pizzas, all the kids stood up and put their hands out for quarters to play video games. Greta, Henry and Lauren were given money and sent on their way, but Mr. Patton asked Jack and Noah to sit down.

They fell back into their seats and crossed their arms. The boys looked like they had lost their dog – or a big baseball game – or found out that summer had been cancelled for the rest of their lives.

"So," Mr. Patton started, "exactly how much money have you earned in the past six weeks?"

Jack was the official accountant, so he spoke. "We have $3,058 to spend on the party already. If we have at least 300 kids at camp the next three weeks, and if slushie sales stay the same, we should end up with way over $7,000."

Noah couldn't contain himself any longer. "And Mom said that whatever we earned we could spend on the party. You can't go changing the rules just because you feel like it. It's not fair!" He gave his dad a mean look.

"I do remember saying that," said Mrs. Patton, "but I didn't think you would earn $7,000. But you have, and now you need to decide how to spend it wisely."

"We are spending it wisely! What do you want us to do? Give it away?" Jack was close to getting grounded.

Greta had just returned to the table for more quarters. "That's the first wise thing you've said all day, Jack. We're supposed to help other people. Don't you listen when you go to church?"

"I listen way more than Dad. He falls asleep all the time."

"I do not sleep during church," replied Mr. Taylor. "I rest my eyes so I can concentrate on the sermon."

"Boys, here are some quarters," said Mrs. Taylor, as she held out her hand. "Go play some video games and think it over."

Jack found an open Ms. Pac Man machine, and started playing. Noah stood behind him, lost in thought while he chewed on a bread stick.

"Snack, why dink for schmerents night night."

"Noah, I didn't know you knew how to speak German."

Noah finished chewing. "Sorry, I don't. But I think our parents and Greta might be right."

"Noah, how can you say that?"

"Maybe spending $7,000 on a birthday party is too much."

Jack gave up on his video game and turned to look at Noah. "How can you do this to me, Noah? We're best friends, and now you're trying to ruin my party too? What happened to you?"

A kid Jack didn't know turned around from another video machine. "You must be the kids I saw on TV tonight. Thanks for making the rest of us kids look so bad. When are you dudes going to get a clue?"

Just then, Mr. Taylor called the kids over to eat. Their table was filled with plates and two huge pizzas. The pizza didn't taste as good to Jack as it usually did. His parents were mad at him, his best friend wasn't on his side anymore, and he was afraid the coolest birthday party ever was never going to happen. He wanted to go home and crawl in bed.

Later that night, Jack was lying in bed when his parents came in to kiss him goodnight.

"What's your thanks to God, Jack?" asked his dad.

"I'm not really sure, Dad." The camp that day had been successful, but the TV story was rotten, and he had argued with adults and kids all night.

Mr. Taylor crouched down and looked at Henry on the bottom bunk bed. "Henry, how about you?"

"My thanks to God are kissing Stella, making paper airplanes and having a water balloon fight with Jack. And pizza."

"Good night, boys," said Mrs. Taylor as she kissed each of them on their foreheads. "I love you."

Jack lay in bed for thirty minutes. He couldn't sleep. He wasn't happy with his parents, he wasn't happy with himself, and the party that was supposed to be fun just didn't seem fun anymore. He got out of bed and found his mom.

"Mom, I'm sad."

"Jack, I know you are. Sometimes this happens when you are successful. Because you've earned so much money, you have more responsibility than you did at the start of the summer, and responsibility isn't always fun. However," and she hugged him, "you and Noah are good boys. I'm sure you'll come up with a good decision."

Noah always went to bed later than Jack, so Jack asked his mom if he could call Noah. They had a short conversation. Noah agreed to clear his schedule for the next three days. Each boy asked his parents if they could work from 9:00 to 5:00 every day the rest of the week. Noah had to skip a book club meeting and hockey practice; Jack cancelled his daily visit to his grandma's house and swore off computer games.

Making a good decision was going to take a lot of time.

28 CHARITABLE THOUGHTS – WEDNESDAY, JULY 23

The boys spent Wednesday at Jack's house to avoid the crowds at Noah's Slushie Stand, although Dirk called occasionally with sales updates. The slushie stand broke its daily sales record by 10:30 and closed at 11:30 after they had sold 176 drinks. Dirk sounded pretty tired during his last call.

Aside from those calls, the Taylor phone didn't ring much anymore, thanks to Greta and Delaney. On Wednesday morning, the girls had sent out an e-mail telling mothers that camp reservations would only be accepted by e-mail for the remainder of the summer. The mothers seemed to like the e-mail option, primarily because it was so difficult to get through on the Taylor phone.

"Noah, I've changed my mind. I think we should give some of our money to charity."

"Me too! I think we should give half to our school."

"Why would we give half to our school? We're surrounded by people who don't have jobs, and you want to give it to our school? Our school has plenty of money."

"Well, I didn't do so well in Science and Social Studies in second grade," said Noah, "and I'm thinking that a big donation might help my grades."

"Noah, that's no better than spending the money on my birthday party. Plus, you know our principal. Do you think we'd get extra favors from her if we gave a big donation?"

"Uh, probably not," replied Noah. "What else do you have in mind?"

"Your mom mentioned the Food Bank. They give free food to people who can't afford it. And my family serves dinner at a homeless shelter, but I can't remember the name. Maybe we should talk to our parents tonight, and talk about this tomorrow."

"OK, so we'll take at least half of the $7,000 and give it to the charities, right?

"That wasn't what I was thinking. I think we need to spend all $7,000 on my birthday party," replied Jack.

"Jack, have you listened to anything that our parents and I have said? We can't spend all of our money on the party. What's the point of picking charities if we spend all the money on the party?"

"You don't understand, Noah. Listen, I spent a lot of time in the bathroom this morning. You know, thinking. I want to use all of our money to throw a huge party – not just for us, but for anyone who wants to come – and then we can raise even more money at the party to give to the charities."

"Are you crazy, Jack? You think we're going to have enough people at the party to raise more money that we already have?"

"That's the dumbest idea I've ever heard," said Greta, as she walked out of the attic closet. "By the way, the lock you put on the attic door isn't very good. Delaney and I had it unlocked in less than ten seconds."

"It is not the dumbest idea ever!" Jack was offended.

"OK, the dumbest idea I've ever heard is jumping off Omaha's tallest building and landing on a couple of mattresses. That's a dumb and dangerous idea. But spending all your money on your party, in the hope of making more money for charity, has to be in the Dumbest Idea Hall of Fame."

Jack turned away from Greta, and looked at Noah, who was eating some old popcorn he'd found in his pocket. "Noah, we can do this. We started with $3 worth of posters. Just imagine how much money we could make for charity if we started with $7,000."

"But we've only got three weeks to do it," argued Noah.

"The Bible says God created the world in seven days." Jack knew that one didn't make sense, but he threw it out anyway.

"It took me three months to read the fourth Harry Potter book," Noah retorted.

"I ate a whole pizza in thirty minutes," said Henry, who had been hiding behind a bookshelf.

"I once laid in bed for twenty hours because I felt like it," added Greta, who really did like to sleep in.

"Woof," barked Stella, who had gotten past the door lock too.

"See, Noah," said Jack, who hadn't proved his point but didn't really care, "three weeks is forever. We could probably build a rocket ship in three weeks. Planning a party in three weeks is, like, well…"

"Eating a whole pizza in thirty minutes," offered Henry.

"Exactly. It's like eating a whole pizza in thirty minutes. We have plenty of time, and we won't be hungry when we're done."

Noah didn't look convinced.

29 WORTHY CAUSES – THURSDAY, JULY 24

Noah arrived late at Jack's house on Thursday morning. "We couldn't get out of our driveway because of all the cars waiting for the slushie stand," complained Noah. "I thought about staying to help out, but Dirk and Turk looked like they were having the time of their lives. By the way, the guys holding the signs on Underwood are dressed up like a dinosaur and a princess today."

"Is the tall kid the princess?" Jack asked as they climbed the stairs to the attic.

"Yep."

"That can't be pretty." Jack paused until they had settled into their office chairs. "So, did you talk to your parents about charities?"

"My mom knew about the homeless shelter where you volunteered, and that's my first choice. It's called the St. Stephen's Mission, a shelter for men, women and children who don't have a place to live. Mom said that a record number of children are living at the shelter this summer, and the shelter needs money for food and beds."

"My dad thinks we should help kids who have cancer. I don't quite understand what cancer is, but you get pretty sick, and most kids do okay after they take a lot of medicine that makes them feel bad. Some kids even have to stay in the hospital for weeks or months at a time, and they might need surgery. My dad helps with a camp, Camp CoHoLo, where kids with cancer can spend three or four days and just be normal again without worrying about being sick. If I had cancer, I think that would be a good place to go."

Jack continued on. "Greta and Delaney have decided that they should help pick a charity because they do so much at camp. They have suggested – well, really, they have demanded – that the Humane Society be one of our charities. Stella even voted for the Humane Society, too, although her bark sounded like it came out of Henry's mouth."

"Was Stella even awake when she supposedly voted for the Humane Society?"

"No way. She was passed out on Henry's bed the entire time we talked about it. Mom took Stella on a four-block walk yesterday, and Stella acted like she had walked to Africa and back."

"Jack, it's impossible to walk all the way to Africa."

"Africa, Australia, Asia, whatever. Wherever, it's a long way to walk."

"You can't walk to… oh, forget it, Jack."

Jack and Noah agreed on the three charities, so then it was time to figure out how to make more money for them. In order to raise a lot of money, they needed to have a really big party. Since they were already running a camp that had over 350 campers and counselors, they decided that they could easily plan a party for over 1,000 people.

"How big of a place do you need for 1,000 people?" Noah wondered.

"Memorial Park holds at least 25,000 people for the July 4th party, so that should be plenty big enough."

Jack wrote a note to his mom asking her to reserve Memorial Park, and then he sent Henry downstairs with the note. Jack was paying Henry five cents for every trip he made downstairs. Sometimes he sent Henry downstairs with blank notes, just to keep him out of the way.

Noah carefully suggested that they change the date of the party. Jack's ninth birthday fell on a Monday, and most adults work on Mondays. Noah didn't want a bunch of adults at the party, but kids needed some way to get there.

Jack had a hard time with this idea. After all, everything they had done so far was focused on Jack's birthday, and now Noah wanted to move the date of the party? Still, after thinking it over, he agreed that more people would come on a Sunday rather than a Monday. The official date of the coolest birthday party ever was changed to Sunday, August 17.

Mrs. Taylor came up several minutes later. "I called the city, and they want to know which part of Memorial Park you want to rent."

Noah was quick to reply. "We want to rent it all."

Mrs. Taylor laughed and responded, "Noah, the park is bigger than a golf course. I don't think you need the whole park."

Noah didn't laugh back. Jack told Mrs. Taylor about the change in dates, and Mrs. Taylor went back downstairs to rent the whole park for August 17th.

Ten minutes later, at 10:30, Jack heard Mrs. Taylor running up the stairs and yelling at the same time. Mrs. Taylor never ran, and she only yelled about elephants. The attic door burst open and Mrs. Taylor finished the final flight of stairs, followed closely by Henry.

"Guys," she panted, "we've got to go. Noah's mom just called. The County Health Department is trying to close down your slushie stand."

30 THE INSPECTOR – THURSDAY, JULY 24 (STILL!)

During the drive to the Patton house, Jack asked his mom what the County Health Department was.

"They do a lot of things to keep all of us healthy, including making sure that restaurants are clean and their food is safe. They check kitchens for bugs, make sure that cooks wash their hands, and stuff like that."

Noah was confused. "Why are they at my house?"

"I'm not sure," said Mrs. Taylor as they turned onto Noah's street, "but I bet they read about you guys in the newspaper last week. Sometimes they don't like people who sell things on the street."

Moms usually liked to exaggerate things, but Mrs. Patton's phone call didn't fully describe what was happening at the slushie stand. Mrs. Taylor had to park her van six houses away because traffic was at a standstill on Noah's street. When they finally reached the house, they saw two health inspectors, dressed in short-sleeve white shirts and ugly ties, standing in front of an even uglier brown car.

Mrs. Patton hadn't mentioned that there were four police cars parked in a half-circle on the street, surrounding the slushie stand. She had also forgotten to describe the group of people who were standing between the police cars and the slushie stand.

In total, there had to be 100 people watching the events at the slushie stand. The ladies from the Christian book club were there, as well as the women from the neighborhood walking club. Other neighbors had come out of their houses when they heard the noise of the crowd, and every little kid within four blocks had followed the police cars to Noah's house.

The dinosaur and princess were late additions, tipped off by the arrival of a fifth police car. Pastor Curtis, taking a break from writing his Sunday sermon, sneaked between the police cars and joined the ladies from the Christian book club. The onlookers also included Noah's little sister Lauren, who saw this as an opportunity to show everyone how well she could dance. She almost cried when one of the police officers asked her to turn off her music.

In the midst of all the bodies and noise, Dirk and Turk were crouched behind the slushie machine. They were hoping that the policemen might not see them, but the arrival of a sixth police car seemed to rule out that possibility.

While baby Meredith was also a strong supporter of the slushie stand, she and Mrs. Patton were locked inside the house. Mrs. Patton had never been in trouble in her life, and she wasn't too excited about spending a night in jail. At first she had opened a window to hear what was going on, but now she was watching the standoff on live television. She could watch it all on television, of course, because there were several TV crews on her front lawn and a TV helicopter was hovering overhead.

The two health inspectors seemed a bit overwhelmed by the crowd. They kept asking the policemen for advice, but the police weren't helping. In fact, once Noah looked closely, he realized that the policemen weren't working for the inspectors. They were only there to make sure no one got hit by a car or started a riot. The policemen probably weren't needed, but two of the police cars had been in line for slushies when the health inspectors arrived. The policemen had called for help when more grandmas arrived. The policemen knew how dangerous grandmas could be.

As the number of onlookers continued to grow, Jack began to fear for the health inspectors' safety. He nudged Noah, and they both walked toward the inspectors. Jack was walking stiffly and seemed to be studying something on the ground as he went past the policemen to reach the inspectors. He looked up and saw that the shorter of the two inspectors seemed downright scared. He was wiping sweat off his forehead with a red cloth, and his eyes kept darting in every direction.

"Excuse me, sir, but did we do something wrong?" asked Jack.

"We need to speak to the adult who is in charge of this food stand," replied the taller inspector, who was Mr. Kraznick according to his nametag.

"We're in charge of this stand, and it's not a food stand. It's a slushie stand," replied Jack.

"I see you're selling cookies, too, so it's a food stand. The County Health Department is in charge of all food stands, and I think your food stand is illegal." Mr. Kraznick crossed his arms and puffed out his chest.

"What's illegal about it? Has anyone gotten sick? Has anyone complained?"

"No one has complained, but it's against the law to have an unlicensed food stand." Kraznick puffed up again.

Jack rubbed his chin. "I have this peddler's license to sell things," as he flashed it at Kraznick, "and we don't actually sell the cookies. When someone has five punches on their Slushie Card, we give them a free cookie. If it's illegal to give away free cookies, then you need to arrest my grandma."

"You still sell those slushies," Kraznick spitted out, clearly frustrated that a little kid was arguing with him, "and slushies are food!" The short inspector was beginning to edge towards his car.

"Sir, a slushie is made of water and powder. I really don't see how that qualifies as food. On top of that, we're running this slushie stand to raise money for charities. Don't you like charities?" Jack waited while Kraznick mumbled something that didn't sound like English. "I don't understand what we're doing wrong. Are you going to give me a ticket or something that says which law I'm breaking?"

"Yes, you bet your life I am! If you open this slushie stand tomorrow, you'll be getting an armful of tickets!" With that, Kraznick stomped away to his car. It was several moments before the short inspector unlocked the door to let him in.

Noah leaned over and said to Jack, "Um, Jack, this isn't good. The last ticket we got from the fire department was $100, and Inspector Kraznick said he's going to give us an armful of tickets. An armful of tickets could cost us over a million dollars."

A newspaper reporter stepped out of the protest circle to talk to Jack and Noah. "Do either of you have a comment?"

"Well, we decided last night that we were going to start giving some of our money to charity. Now it sounds like we might have to give a bunch of the money to the County Health Department."

"So what are you going to do?"

"I'm really not sure," said Jack, and he cocked his head to think. "But I'm leaning towards going swimming. It's way too hot to go play at the park this afternoon."

31 EMERGENCY MEETING – THURSDAY, JULY 24

The health inspector had threatened to ticket the boys if they opened their stand on Friday. After he returned from swimming, Jack called his dad at work to see if he should hire a lawyer.

Mr. Taylor called his lawyer friend again, and Mr. Dooley agreed to work for free if Jack bought him dinner at Mama's Pizza that night. At 6:00, the Taylors, the Pattons, and John Dooley, attorney-at-law, met to discuss the serious legal problems of two soon-to-be third graders. Jack couldn't help but notice, as they drove by on the way to Mama's, that the homeless shelter seemed busier than ever.

Mrs. Patton asked Greta, Henry and Lauren to play video games while the attorney talked to the boys. Greta refused to leave the table. She crossed her arms and said, "I'm not going anywhere! If my brother is going to jail, I'm going too." Henry and Lauren crossed their arms too. Baby Meredith also made a grumpy face, but she probably just had gas.

Mr. Dooley spoke up. "I could always use more help on this case, and Greta seems pretty sharp."

He then turned to the boys. "I've gone to the Health Department's website to see what rules you might be breaking. Your peddler's license was probably only good for the July 4th party, so I had Noah's dad get another license today for the slushie stand."

Noah interrupted Mr. Dooley. "So now we're legal, right? The health inspector can't arrest us anymore?"

Mr. Dooley shook his head, but Greta interrupted him before he could speak. "I've been doing a little Internet research as well," she began. "The health inspector might still be able to do something. The peddler's license allows you to sell things, but the Health Department has more rules if you're selling food. The big question is whether a slushie is food, and whether you're making them in a safe way. I'm sure that the inspector will argue that you're breaking the law."

Mrs. Patton was usually quiet, but not when she's mad. "He thinks I don't make them in a safe way? I scrub the machine and buckets every night – I wash my hands and wear gloves when I make them – my house is spotless!" Mrs. Patton had a red face. Noah got a little scared.

Mr. Dooley put his hands up in front of his body, as if Mrs. Patton might attack him. "Please understand, I know how clean you are. But Greta is correct. By tomorrow morning, you need to have a typed memo describing how you clean the tubs and buckets, and how you make the slushies…"

Greta interrupted Mr. Dooley again. "I performed an Internet search for slushie stands – do you know that there are huge companies that sell slushies in malls? – and some County Health departments do think that slushies qualify as food. However, there are also a lot of gas stations in Omaha that sell slushies, and the County Health department leaves them alone."

Mr. Dooley felt like he needed to earn his pizza, so he interrupted Greta. "You should also make sure that Dirk and Turk take a shower tomorrow morning. I saw them on television today, and they're looking pretty gross. However, even if you do all of these things, the inspector will probably still give you several tickets just because he can. He could even decide to close down your slushie stand and take away your slushie machine."

"Does it matter that we're going to give some of the money to a charity?" asked Noah.

Mr. Dooley shook his head. "No, the County Health department doesn't care what you do with the money. They only care about how food is prepared."

Mr. Taylor looked a little worried. "What are the chances they'll get arrested?"

"Thanks, Dad, for not wanting me to go to jail."

"Oh, Jack, I'm not worried about you going to jail. It's just that you have a lot of chores at home that you haven't done this week, and I need to know if you're going to be around the rest of the week to get them done. If you're going to be arrested, we really need to get those chores done tonight."

"I'm sorry, Jack," said Mrs. Taylor. "Dad's just kidding. If anyone goes to jail, it should be him for telling bad jokes."

Despite all the advice from Mr. Dooley and Greta, the boys weren't feeling any better by the time the pizzas arrived. The boys' parents and Mr. Dooley started talking about some famous movie star who had gotten into trouble, and the boys concentrated on eating pizza. At 7:00, Mr. Dooley left, but not before telling Jack and Noah that he would be at the slushie stand the next morning.

He would have plenty of company.

32 EARLY MORNINGS STINK – FRIDAY, JULY 25

Noah and Jack had gotten used to avoiding the slushie stand the past two weeks, so they weren't looking forward to spending Friday there. Of course, the risk of being arrested was also a pretty good reason to not go there but, after all, it was <u>their</u> slushie stand.

The health inspector had yelled his last comment yesterday, "If you open this slushie stand tomorrow, you'll be getting an armful of tickets." Because he yelled it, the TV cameras had captured his voice. Because he yelled it at two eight-year-olds, Omaha's four TV stations played the video repeatedly on Thursday night and Friday morning.

Fortunately, the TV stations had also captured one of Jack's comments - "…we're running this slushie stand to raise money for charities. Don't you like charities?" Because of this, nearly everyone in Omaha thought the health inspector was picking on

Jack and Noah. When Jack and Greta got out of bed at 6:30 a.m. – ugh, 6:30! - Mrs. Taylor was flipping between radio stations, listening to people talk about the slushie stand. About the only person on the inspector's side seemed to be one guy who called into the radio station. He owned a gas station, and because of Jack and Noah, his slushie sales were now horrible on Wednesday, Thursday and Friday.

Channel 7 had a live interview with Mr. Dooley at 7:00 a.m. in front of Noah's house. The newspaper had interviewed the health inspector, the mayor and the governor about the slushie stand. The newspaper had tried to reach Jack and Noah's second grade teacher, but she was on vacation. Their school principal refused to give interviews, primarily because she thought the two boys wouldn't be coming back to school in August – she figured they'd be in jail by then.

A Channel 6 reporter interviewed a food expert who listed eight health department rules that he thought Jack and Noah were breaking. The expert predicted a $2,000 fine, the closing of the slushie stand, and up to 90 days in jail. Greta tried to call the TV station to argue with the food expert, but Mr. Taylor made her hang up the phone.

The entire Taylor family arrived at the Patton house at 7:30, and Mr. Patton welcomed them at the door.

"How about that?" said Mr. Patton, "I didn't expect to see Mr. Taylor here too."

"It's not every day that your oldest child gets arrested for the first time, Mr. Patton," Mr. Taylor replied. "I've got two cameras, one video camera, and I've asked Greta to do some crayon drawings of the scene where the boys get arrested."

"I know what you mean," said Mr. Patton, as he winked at Greta. "I made Noah wear a shirt with a collar. If they're going to take a picture of him at the police station, it might be good enough to use for our Christmas cards."

"A clean t-shirt would have been fine," grumped Noah, who nodded his head to Jack. It wasn't a particularly friendly welcome, but neither Noah nor Jack had slept much the previous night. Both Noah and Jack were worried that they wouldn't be sleeping at home for a while.

All four television stations had cameras in place by 8:00 a.m. Four police cars arrived at 8:15 to help with crowd control. Mr. Patton brought the water hose around to the front of the house in case he needed to put out any fires. He couldn't imagine why there would be a fire, but there was a rumor that Crazy Luke might be coming. At 8:30, Mrs. Patton, Mrs. Taylor and Meredith got into Mrs. Patton's car and drove to the police station. Mrs. Taylor thought it was important to have someone at the police station when the boys were taken there.

At 8:45, Dirk's buddies arrived to pick up their signs. They really weren't needed today, because everyone in Omaha knew that the slushie stand was open. However, the two guys were dressed as a giant ladybug and a pink banana, and Jack didn't have the heart to tell them to go home.

Dirk and Turk were nervous. They were both hoping to get into good high schools, and they thought that getting arrested might hurt their chances. Even worse, their mom and dad couldn't afford to pay a ticket or hire a lawyer. Noah sent them to play video games in his basement.

At 9:00, Jack, Noah, Henry, Greta, Lauren, Mr. Taylor and Mr. Patton stood in the garage. Jack grabbed the wagon handle, nodded to Mr. Patton, and the garage door began to open. As he pulled the wagon to the end of the driveway, Jack's legs started to get weak. He lost his balance, tripped over Noah's foot, and went sprawling over the slushie machine and wagon, which both followed him to the pavement.

There had to be at least 500 people standing in the street, and they all gasped in horror. Jack was flat on the driveway covered in five gallons of cherry and strawberry slushie. He didn't like the way the day was starting.

33 YOUR BROTHER GEORGE – FRIDAY, JULY 25

Dads aren't particularly helpful when it comes to cleaning up a mess, but Mr. Taylor and Mr. Patton did the best they could. Jack first went to the backyard, where Mr. Patton washed him off with a garden hose. Noah came out with a new set of clothes for Jack to wear, and Jack dripped into the bathroom to change. Meanwhile, Mr. Taylor pulled the slushie machine back into the garage, cleaned it as well as he knew how – certainly not up to Mrs. Patton's standards, but still good enough – and then he dumped in two more buckets of slushies.

At 9:12, Jack, Noah, Henry, Greta, Lauren, Mr. Taylor and Mr. Patton stood in the garage. Jack grabbed the wagon handle, nodded to Mr. Patton, and the garage door began to open. This time, though, Noah took the wagon handle from Jack, and he pulled the wagon next to the street. Jack made sure the power cord was still plugged in, and they both tried to ignore the TV cameras, policemen and crowd. To Jack's left, Noah organized empty cups and cookies on a folding table. Once everything was in place, they both looked up to see whether the crowd was filled with customers or enemies.

"Noah's Slushie Stand is now open for business," Noah yelled.

Almost immediately, a line formed. Pastor Curtis was first, and after he blessed the slushie stand, he told Noah that he was always available if the boys needed help choosing a charity or two. He was followed by Mrs. Churchill and the Christian book club ladies. Mrs. Churchill leaned over Noah when she got to the front of the line and whispered, "Noah, don't worry about giving me an elephant ride. I'm so proud of you for giving your slushie money to charity. If you need any help, you just let me know."

After the book club came the neighborhood walking club and the Benson High School marching band – or at least sixty of its members. Dirk and Turk had said that the marching band had stopped the last two mornings while practicing for a big competition. Today they were wearing their uniforms. Jack figured the band director knew they would be on TV.

The TV cameras might also have been the reason for the ten college kids in line behind the band. They were dressed up as characters from Star Wars. Luke Skywalker and Darth Vader were fighting with plastic light sabers, and Princess Leia screamed every time Luke was hit. The Stormtroopers looked very bored while holding their fake white rifles, but the real policemen kept an eye on them just to be safe.

The line moved quickly once Mr. Patton and Mr. Taylor started helping. Greta and Henry handed out free cookies with every sale. The marching band started playing songs, and Lauren danced with a police officer in the yard. By 10:00, they had sold 200 slushies, and Mr. Taylor was refilling the tubs about every ten minutes. Mr. Dooley, who was now being paid in slushies and cookies rather than pizza, came out of the house from his third bathroom break and headed straight for the boys.

"Jack and Noah," he said, "unless someone else wants to interview me, I'm probably going to leave in a few minutes."

"That's fine, Mr. Dooley," Greta said, without looking up from the cookie table. "I'll do all the lawyer work for the rest of the day. I've totally got it covered."

Mr. Dooley drove off at 10:05, and everything was going great. Well, it was until 10:10, when Luke Skywalker came running up to the stand. "The Empire is attacking, my brave friends," gasped Luke. "Even with my best fighting, I cannot keep the health inspector from coming." Luke bowed and ran away into the crowd, with Darth Vader close behind. Princess Leia took her place behind Noah. He tried to remain calm, but it didn't help that Princess Leia shrieked every ten seconds.

About fifty yards away, Jack could see the crowd parting for a group of people. Health Inspector Kraznick led the group, and four very serious men in suits were behind him. The short health inspector from yesterday was nowhere to be seen.

When Kraznick reached the opposite side of the street, two police officers stopped him. "Why are you here, Kraznick?" asked Sergeant Hillman, who was still sweating from his dance with Lauren.

"I'm here to ticket those two kids for running an illegal slushie stand. It's my job to make sure everyone follows the law," Kraznick replied, "and no one is going to stop me from doing my job."

Sergeant Hillman leaned toward Inspector Kraznick and whispered, "That's fine, Inspector, but I think you're outnumbered."

Kraznick shot back, "Well, you're the police. Get them out of my way!" Princess Leia screamed again and pretended to faint into Han Solo's arms.

No one was buying slushies anymore, so Noah, Jack and Greta were watching Inspector Kraznick and Sergeant Hillman. "What do we do now?" asked Noah. "I don't want to be the cause of a riot. Our jail sentence might be even longer then."

"Relax, boys, I think we just need to have a talk with Inspector Kraznick. Follow me." Greta walked over to where Sergeant

Hillman and Inspector Kraznick were standing. Jack guessed that the two men were at least three feet taller than Greta.

"Inspector Kraznick, I am Greta Taylor, and I represent the two boys who own this slushie stand. Would you be so kind as to tell me exactly what laws these boys are breaking?"

"You're too young to understand."

"I've been reading up on the health department rules. Talk really slow and maybe I'll understand."

"First, they are violating County Health Code section 142(a), subsection 17(b), by serving food outdoors without proper health protections," Inspector Kraznick began.

"But Inspector Kraznick, you can clearly see that there are metal lids on the top of the slushie machine. Nothing can get into the slushie mix. I don't think section 142(a), subsection 17(b) has been violated."

Inspector Kraznick's head jerked back a bit. "OK, then they are violating County Health Code section 138(b), which regulates how food can be transported outdoors."

"Inspector Kraznick, section 138(b) only applies to companies that make sausages. You should know that."

"They are violating County Health Code section 115(d), which requires that all food must be prepared in a clean room. They're making slushies in a garage."

"Inspector Kraznick, Mrs. Patton prepares the slushie mix in her kitchen. If you can find a restaurant that is cleaner than Mrs. Patton's kitchen, then I'll give up chocolate for the rest of my life. We clearly meet the requirements of section 115(d)."

"They are also violating…" Kraznick continued, but was interrupted by Greta.

"Mr. Kraznick, could we have a private conversation, maybe over there?" Greta asked, as she pointed to a quiet spot near the police cars.

"Um, sure, but I want you policemen to watch her every move," he said, talking to Sergeant Hillman. Sergeant Hillman rolled his eyes, and started arguing with his partner about the best slushie flavor.

When they were away from the crowd of people, Greta leaned in towards Inspector Kraznick. He had to bend over to hear her. "Mr. Kraznick, we both know that Jack and Noah aren't breaking any rules. And… we both know why you're doing this."

"I don't know what you mean, little girl."

"I just figured it out. I mean, you look familiar, but I've never seen you before today. Then, when I got up this morning, I heard your brother talking on the radio. He had called a radio show to complain about the slushie stand."

"I don't know what you're talking about," Inspector Kraznick said, but he wouldn't look Greta in the eye anymore.

169

"You see, my parents have used the same gas station since I was a baby – it's called George's Gas Station – and this guy George has been the owner of it for as long as I can remember. I suppose that's why they call it 'George's Gas Station.' And then I recognized his voice on the radio today, and that made me remember seeing his name on a certificate on the wall of the gas station. His full name is George Kraznick. I can't tell you why I remembered his last name, but I guess it's because it sounds so weird."

"Our name is not… I mean, I've never met him. He must be a distant relative."

"He sure looks a lot like you." Greta paused. "And then I remembered how Jack knew about slushies. He used to buy them at George's Gas Station. But now he doesn't. On the radio, George said that a lot of people don't buy slushies from him anymore."

Inspector Kraznick wasn't talking anymore.

"So I think we should make a deal. That's what my dad says when Mom doesn't agree with him. They make deals. Anyway, here's my deal. I'm the only one here who knows that George is your brother, or cousin, or whatever he is. You're the only one here who can give Jack and Noah a ticket. If you leave the boys alone, I won't tell anyone about George, and the slushie stand will close in three weeks when the boys go back to school."

Inspector Kraznick was looking at his car. He wanted to leave. Greta waited for an answer.

"OK, since you're not saying anything, we must have a deal. Let's shake hands, and it will look like we made an official agreement."

At that point, Inspector Kraznick would have done a back flip if Greta insisted on it. They shook hands, he walked straight to his car, and he was out of sight within a minute.

Greta turned to the crowd, and gave a thumbs-up sign with both hands. Sergeant Hillman lifted Greta onto his shoulders, the Benson High School band played "We Are the Champions," and the crowd roared its approval.

Above all the noise, Jack and Noah yelled together, "NOAH'S SLUSHIE STAND IS OPEN FOR BUSINESS!"

34 UNCOMFORTABLE DISCUSSION – FRIDAY, JULY 25

Mrs. Patton, Mrs. Taylor and Meredith returned from the police station shortly after 11:00, happy that the boys hadn't been arrested, but a little annoyed that there were still two TV cameras and about 500 people in front of the house. The slushie stand remained open until 12:15, and Jack, Noah and Greta signed autographs until 12:30. None of them were that good at writing in cursive, especially when they had to autograph a baby's forehead. Still, it was nice to feel famous for a day.

Jack and Noah's dads had taken a vacation day from work so they could watch the boys get arrested. Since that didn't quite work out, the parents decided that they should use the time to get the boys organized. After the slushie stand closed, the Pattons and Taylors met in the Patton's backyard.

"OK, boys, so do you still think you're going to have about $7,000 to spend on the party?" asked Mr. Taylor.

"Well, if the slushie stand stays this busy, it will probably be more like $11,000 or $12,000," Noah replied.

"And I think not getting arrested should help our attendance at the last three summer camps. We really need to get 400 kids at the next camp, because the Amazing Arthur said he wouldn't do the last two shows if we have less than 400."

"I'm also thinking about opening a lawyer office next week," added Greta. "That could add a few thousand dollars."

"This is starting to be too much to handle," said Mrs. Taylor. She turned to Greta. "I'm sorry, honey, but you can't open a lawyer office. We can only have two businesses at once and, let's face it, you're the one running the summer camp."

"So," Mrs. Patton asked, "based on what you've been telling the newspaper and TV stations, it sounds like you two have agreed that you're giving almost all of the money to a charity?"

"Actually…. no, we're not giving any of that money to charity," Jack squeaked, barely loud enough to be heard over the birds chirping overhead.

"Excuse me, but I must have heard you wrong. It sounded like you said that you were keeping the money for yourself," said Mr. Taylor, in a not-very-nice voice.

Noah took a deep breath. "Yes, that's right. We're not giving any of <u>that</u> money to charity."

35 GAME PLAN – FRIDAY, JULY 25

"Before you get too mad at us," started Jack, "give us a chance to explain. Noah and I talked about this for an hour last night, and we think we have a really good plan. Will you at least listen to it?"

Four parents were looking at Jack and Noah, and none of them looked very happy. No one talked for an awkward thirty seconds. To Jack, it seemed like six years. Mr. and Mrs. Taylor spent the time looking up at the sky and mumbling to the clouds. They seemed to do that a lot recently.

Finally, Mr. Taylor said, "So, Jack, instead of donating most of the money to charity, you still want to waste it on your birthday party?"

"No, Dad, I don't want to waste it on a party. I want to throw a party that will make even more money, and then we'll give everything we make to charity." Jack took a deep breath. "And it's no longer my birthday party. It's a birthday party for the entire city."

Mr. Patton jumped into the discussion. "Boys, I'm really impressed with how much money you've earned the last eight weeks, but how are you going to make money throwing a party?"

"It's easy, Dad," replied Noah. "If we make the party really fun, and then we ask for donations, everyone will give money."

The boys handed out copies of their ideas to the four parents. The details included:

- *2-mile race around Memorial Park at 8:00 a.m.*
- *Pancake Man serving breakfast at 9:00 a.m.*
- *Cow races (with riders) at 10:00 a.m.*
- *Homemade airplane races at 11:00 a.m. (real airplanes, not paper ones)*
- *Soccer tournament for kids beginning at noon*
- *Most-people-in-a-car competition at 1:00*
- *Motorcycle stunt man at 2:00 p.m.*
- *Performers from the Omaha Magician's Society all afternoon*
- *Concert beginning at 3:00 p.m.*
- *Strongest man competition at 4:00 p.m.*
- *Bounce houses (because kids love bounce houses) and lots of clowns all day*
- *Huge fireworks show at 10:00 p.m.*

The boys had other ideas too, but they weren't sure all of them would work.

Mr. Taylor wasn't sure about their plan, but he was willing to help. "Boys," he said, "in order for this to be successful, you're going to need a lot of people there. Maybe you should hold a press conference this weekend, while the TV stations are still interested in you. How about 2:00 on Sunday?"

"That's my nap time," piped in Henry, who was sitting under Mr. Taylor's chair. "How about 4:00 instead?"

"I sure hope it goes better than the first time I was on TV," remarked Jack. "I'm tired of being called 'that selfish kid' when I go to the swimming pool."

36 THE PRESS CONFERENCE – SUNDAY, JULY 27

Neither Jack nor Noah had ever held a press conference. Come to think of it, the only time they'd seen one was when a quarterback or a coach was interviewed after a big football game. After lunch on Sunday, Jack paced back and forth so much in the backyard that he wore out a patch of grass. Stella was offended; it was her job to kill the grass in the backyard.

Noah arrived at 2:00 p.m. to prepare for the press conference. They went to Mrs. Taylor for help.

"Why don't you just write down what you want to say? I've seen a lot of press conferences where people started by first reading from a sheet of paper." She didn't tell Jack this, but she also thought that reading from a piece of paper might stop Jack from throwing up for at least a few minutes.

At 4:01 p.m., Jack walked out the back door of his house and took his seat behind a folding table that Mr. Taylor had put in the back yard. Stella was licking the leg of a cameraman, and Henry was running around the yard taking pictures with a fake camera. Jack counted four cameras, and six microphones had been placed on the table. There were about a dozen strangers in the back yard.

Mr. Taylor announced, "Jack Taylor will begin the press conference by reading a statement. Please hold your questions until he is finished." Jack began reading:

"Noah Patton and I would like to thank you for coming to my house. Today we would like to announce that on Sunday, August 17, we are going to have a birthday party for all of Omaha at Memorial Park. There will be no charge to attend the party, but we will be accepting donations."

"All of the money we collect will be donated to three charities. Our families have been involved in all three charities, and we think that they will put our money to good use. The three charities are the St. Stephen's Mission, the Nebraska Humane Society and Camp CoHoLo."

"In the past seven weeks, Noah and I have earned over $4,000. We have two goals. First, we want to raise at least $20,000 to give to these charities. Second, we want everyone to have fun at Omaha's birthday party. For one day we'd like everyone to forget their problems and have a good time."

"We hope at least 5,000 people will come to the party. We know that some adults don't believe that we can plan a party that big, but we know we can do it. To prove that we can do some pretty big things, please direct your attention to the driveway."

The four cameras and all heads turned towards the driveway. There was nothing there. The back yard was quiet, but then several car horns were heard in front of the house. A large shadow fell on the driveway and then, with soft thuds, an elephant came into view.

Henry whooped with joy. Mrs. Patton screamed in terror. Stella pulled at her leash, determined to eat the elephant for an early dinner. Meanwhile, the cameras kept filming, and eventually they focused on the 8-year-old boy sitting on top of the elephant – Noah Patton.

Noah clapped twice, and the elephant kneeled down. Noah climbed over the elephant's head and slid down the trunk to the ground. With another clap from Noah, the elephant rose, turned, and walked down the driveway out of sight. Noah walked to the folding table and sat down.

He looked at the cameras and said, "I would like to announce a fourth charity for Omaha's birthday party. We will also be raising money for the Nebraska Wildlife Shelter, a shelter that takes care of old circus animals. The shelter's five elephants will be giving elephant rides at the party for $5 each."

"While we know that not everyone will be able to take an elephant ride, we're pretty sure that everyone can have a turn in a bounce house. We have arranged for 25 bounce houses to be at the park that day. Let's see – 25 bounce houses with six kids each – that's 150 kids bouncing at one time."

Jack started again. "We are also searching for several bands to play at the party. A crowd of at least 5,000 people seems like a great place for a band to play."

Noah distributed the party's schedule of events to the reporters, starting with the 8:00 a.m. race. The reporters asked a few small questions, but none of them were hard. Mr. Taylor had predicted that would happen. When reporters see an elephant in someone's driveway, they tend to forget what they were going to ask.

37 STAR POWER – TUESDAY, JULY 29

The seventh session of Noah and Jack's Summer Camp was held on July 29 at Elmwood Park. Since the previous Tuesday, the boys had been involved in a televised showdown with the County Health Inspector, held a press conference and, by the way, sold over 700 slushies. Nearly all of the television stories and newspaper articles about Noah's Slushie Stand had mentioned the summer camp, so last week's record of 324 campers was sure to be broken. The Amazing Arthur would get his audience of 400 kids after all.

A Boy Scout troop was enlisted to provide crowd control, and Rachel recruited more Girl Scouts to serve as camp counselors. Greta and Delaney were promoted to camp directors, which seemed a bit odd since they were only seven years old, but they'd already been doing the job since the second camp. Plus, Jack and

Noah were too busy planning a party to spend much time on camp.

Fortunately, Greta and Delaney knew – as all little girls do – how to tell people what to do, and the camp went well. The campers went through 59 gallons of lemonade, 36 boxes of Oreo's, and three tall containers of those wet napkins that you use when you get sticky.

Henry thought the counselors were giving out too many Oreo's, but he had to admit that 523 kids do tend to eat a lot of cookies. Henry tried to count all the money from camp, but the number got too big. Delaney and Greta took over, and counted over $3,000.

📖 📖 📖 📖 📖 📖 📖 📖

While everyone else was running the summer camp, Jack and Noah were trying to improve their party. Jack had met Charles Compton, a professional basketball player, at a basketball camp he attended last year, and he wanted Charles to come to the party. Noah used the Internet to find a phone number for Charles' basketball team, and Jack called. Jack talked to a very nice grandma who answered the phone, and he explained what he wanted.

After Jack hung up the phone, he e-mailed the grandma copies of the recent newspaper articles about the party. He also sent the basketball grandma the address of the website that Greta and Delaney had created for the party. The boys couldn't figure out how the girls knew so much about computers, but Greta and Delaney were pretty good at it.

Noah called the Disney Channel and provided the same information to another grandma who answered the phone. Noah didn't really care who came from the Disney Channel – they were all pretty cool – but he asked for Disney's biggest star, Mandy Peters. He had read on the Internet that Mandy loved elephants, so he made sure to e-mail the grandma the newspaper picture where he was riding the elephant. He also autographed the picture, because that's what famous people do.

Finally, Jack called his cousin Daniel in Colorado. Daniel did tricks with skis and snowboards, and he knew a lot of people who did cool things like that. Jack asked Daniel to find a motorcycle stuntman for the party. For some reason, it took Daniel a few minutes to realize that Jack was being serious.

38 GETTING EXCITED – FRIDAY, AUGUST 1

After a lunch of grilled cheese sandwiches and warm chocolate chip cookies, Jack and Noah headed back to their office in Jack's attic.

"It's been a good week. We had 523 kids at camp on Tuesday, and we – er, I mean Greta – didn't lose one of them," commented Jack, with a little bit of surprise in his voice.

"And Dirk and Turk have been busy at the slushie stand. They sold over 1,000 slushies this week. I gave them a $20 bonus," added Noah.

"What were the poster guys wearing this week?"

"A flamingo, a bear, a marshmallow and a piece of toast were my favorites. Do you know that a costume shop is sponsoring those guys now? The costume shop pays them more than we do."

Noah shook his head. "It seems everyone is doing something crazy now."

"The money is adding up, that's for sure," remarked Jack. "Here's our profit ledger after this morning's slushie sales," and he handed Noah the paper, which seemed a little less official since Jack had written everything with a purple crayon.

Parent money	$45
Allowance money	50
Camp June 17	(3)
Camp June 24	(20)
Camp July 1	309
Necklace sales, July 4	(295)
Camp July 8	327
Slushie stand, July 9 – 11	(23)
Camp July 15	358
Slushie stand July 16 – 18	587
Camp July 22	1,723
Slushie stand July 23 – 25	1,289
Camp July 29	2,745
Slushie stand July 30 – Aug 1	1,892
Total	$8,984

Jack also told Noah that one of their three phone calls from Tuesday had paid off. Cousin Daniel called yesterday to say that one of his buddies knew a guy, Slash Stevens, who competed in the X Games in motorcycle racing. His grandma lived in Omaha, and he would arrange a visit around the birthday party. Jack offered to pay Slash, but Slash turned him down. When Slash was a kid, his best friend had cancer, so Slash wanted to help the kids' cancer camp by performing for free.

"Have you heard anything from Charles Compton?" Noah asked for the fifth time in two days.

"No, and I doubt we will. My dad said that famous people aren't going to drop everything to come to Omaha just because we asked."

"Should we leave another message for him?"

"I don't think so," said Jack. "I've called Charles so many times that the grandma answering the phone recognizes my voice. I don't think she's delivering my messages anymore."

"Well, it's not all bad. We've got three bands from Omaha that want to play at our concert," said Noah, and he read from a list that he pulled from his hat. "We've got 'Bunny Thumpers,' 'Washed-Up Cowboys,' and 'Completely Normal.'"

"Are they any good?" Jack had never heard any of them on the radio.

Noah nodded. "My dad listened to their music, and he said they were pretty good. They dress weird, though. My mom says she can't understand how the bands can walk around in public dressed like that, but Dad called her a 'huddy-muddy' or something like that."

"What's a huddy-muddy?"

"I think it's someone who's boring. Anyway, the Creighton University basketball team has offered to sign autographs, but I said 'no.'"

"You said what?" Jack was a huge fan of the Creighton basketball team, and was dying to meet the players.

"Relax," said Noah. "I told the coach what I really wanted were ten autographed basketballs so we could auction them for charity. Greta has an auction page set up on our website. You know, you really ought to take computer lessons from Greta. She's way smarter than you."

"Thanks, Noah. That's nice to hear, especially from my best friend." He paused. "You know, we're getting a lot of stuff done, but we've got to do more. We've got to do something to make people more excited about the party."

"Come on, Jack," Noah replied, "our party has been in the newspaper, on the TV and radio, and everyone in Omaha is talking about it. Don't you think they're excited enough?"

"That's the problem, Noah. The only people who are talking about it are people who live in Omaha. If we want to get Charles and Mandy here, we've got to get people everywhere excited about the party."

"How in the heck do you do that, Jack? We hardly know anyone outside of Omaha except our cousins, and that's maybe fifty people. Plus, we only have sixteen days until the party."

Jack leaned back and smiled. "It's easy, Noah. We just need to talk to Greta and Delaney. If we put something on the Internet, everyone in the world will know about it."

39 MOVIE STARS – SATURDAY, AUGUST 2

Delaney and Greta had refused to meet with the boys on Friday afternoon. The girls were in the middle of playing school when Jack knocked on Greta's bedroom door, and a little while later they all left for the swimming pool. It was summer, after all.

Greta agreed that they would meet with the boys at 10:00 a.m. on Saturday. Noah wanted to meet at 8:00, but Greta insisted on sleeping until 9:00 on Saturday mornings. Greta was often busy during the week, and she needed at least one lazy morning.

The meeting started in Greta's room promptly at, well, 10:30. Apparently Greta needed a little more sleep than usual. Jack talked while Delaney and Greta sent e-mails on their laptops.

"OK, girls. We need to create excitement for the party. Most of the people in Omaha know about it, but we want it to be so popular that Mandy Peters will want to be here."

Greta laughed. "Mandy Peters? Are you kidding me? She hasn't left California in three years. People Magazine said that her mom is afraid of flying, so they never leave Hollywood."

Jack was frustrated. "Forget Mandy Peters. Forget anyone famous. We just want to put something on the Internet that talks about the party. Something that people will notice."

Delaney shook her head, and frowned like a teacher. "Jack, the Internet is huge. Just because you put something on the Internet doesn't mean people will notice it. It has to be funny, or unusual, or cool."

"Yeah, Jack," interrupted Greta. "Like the movies Dad made last year when he grew a mustache to raise money for Camp CoHoLo. He gave his mustache a funny name, and then he made movies about it. Remember the music video? The one where you only saw his mouth and mustache, and it looked like he was singing those funny songs. About 10,000 people saw his video on YouTube."

"Blue scuba?" Noah was confused.

"Noah," Greta said, as she shook her head, "how is it that you're eight years old and you don't know these things? YouTube is a website where anybody can put a video, and then everybody else can watch it. It's one of the most popular websites in the world."

Delaney nodded and turned to the boys. "That's totally what you should do. You make a funny video. But it has to be funny. If it's not funny, Greta and I refuse to be part of it. If we decide it's funny, we'll e-mail everyone we know – plus the 500 moms on our camp list – and tell them to forward the link to the video to all their friends. If everyone keeps forwarding the link, eventually people outside Omaha will know about it. After that, who knows?"

Noah threw up his hands. "Great. First we earn almost $9,000 in two months. Then we plan the biggest birthday party in Omaha's history. And now we have to make a funny movie. Whatever happened to just being a kid?"

Jack stood up and patted Noah on his head. "Being a kid? You can be a kid next summer. This summer we need to be movie stars."

📖 📖 📖 📖 📖 📖 📖 📖

The boys wasted no time in tracking down Mr. Taylor in the backyard. He was mowing the grass while Stella, the usually lazy basset hound, barked and circled the lawnmower for no apparent reason.

Still sweating from the hot August morning, Mr. Taylor collapsed into a lawn chair. The boys moved their chairs next to him.

Jack leaned towards his dad. "Ok, Dad, so here's the deal. We want to make a funny movie, like you did with your mustache, so that more people will know about the party. We decided that you could help us with ideas and filming and making it and a bunch of other stuff."

"That sounds like a lot of work," Mr. Taylor replied. "I write, direct, film and produce it. What exactly do you two plan to do?"

"We're going to be the actors," said Noah. "Acting is the hardest part anyway. We'll have to memorize our lines, comb our hair, maybe even put on make-up."

Jack sat up in his chair. "Hold it right there, Noah, I'm not putting on make-up."

"Don't worry about it, Jack. All the big stars put on make-up. It makes you look better on camera. I saw it on a TV show."

Mr. Taylor interrupted the pretty-boy talk. "Boys, I'll help you, but you need to do more than just act. The first thing you need to do is brainstorm about funny ideas."

"Brainstorm?" Jack looked frightened. "What the heck is that?"

Mr. Taylor leaned back in his chair. "Relax. Brainstorming is something I learned about in fifth grade. It's a way for you to be creative, to come up with a bunch of ideas really quickly. You write down every idea you can think of, without deciding whether the idea is good or bad. After you've made a long list, you go back and decide which ideas might be worth keeping."

"Oh, sure, we did some brainstorming when we made the list of things to do at the party. But it was really just a list of things we wanted to do."

"With brainstorming, you try to think of as many ideas as you can, even if they're totally crazy. I'll give you an example. Let's say that I'm in charge of naming a dog. The name has to be two words, and the first word has to start with the letter 'L'. So I just start saying what comes to my mind: Lucky Dog. Lulu Blue. Larry Lee. Linus Bucks. Loopy Lips. Elroy Gunshot."

"Wait, that last one started with an 'E,'" Jack remarked.

"Good catch," Mr. Taylor said, "but it doesn't matter. We're brainstorming. There are no wrong answers. Lovey Dovey. Lake Superior."

Jack and Noah joined in.

"Loaf of Bread."

"Night Light."

"Lady Luck."

"Left Right."

"Little Feet."

"Little Nose."

"Little Chance."

"You've got it boys. Now go to work on your movie."

40 NEARLY FAMOUS – WEDNESDAY, AUGUST 6

For three days, Jack and Noah made list after list of things they thought were funny. Noah snuck a pencil into church and had a list of nearly twenty things by the time the sermon was over. They went to the pool on Sunday and Monday afternoon, but spent all their time in lawn chairs brainstorming while Greta wrote down their ideas.

They spent most of their time at Tuesday's camp videotaping campers saying silly things. The camera died after an hour, so they started making more lists. Delaney begged them for help.

"Come on guys, can you help with snacks? We have over 600 kids today."

"Delaney," replied Jack, "we are in the middle of being geniuses. We can't be bothered with simple things like handing out Oreos. It might stop us from thinking up creative things."

"That's funny, because I just thought of a few creative things I could do to you. Unfortunately, I'd get in trouble if I did them. Thanks for all your help." She stomped away.

Even without the boys' help, the camp went well. With the addition of the Christian book club (Noah took Mrs. Churchill up on her offer to help) and the walking club from Noah's neighborhood (what is better exercise than chasing kids?) as new counselors, Greta was now in charge of eighty camp counselors. Thunderclouds appeared near the end of camp, and tornado sirens began blaring just as Mike Douglas led the campers in the last song, "My Hamster Plays a Guitar." The sirens simply made the camp even more memorable for the 673 kids who attended. After expenses, the day's profit was $3,631.

📖 📖 📖 📖 📖 📖 📖 📖

On Wednesday morning, Jack and Noah met at Noah's house to make sure that Dirk and Turk had the slushie stand under control. The boys had decided on Monday to buy a brand new slushie maker, and Dirk hired two more teenagers to keep both slushie machines filled. Dirk and Turk expanded the hours from 9:00 a.m. to 1:00 p.m., and the costume shop was now paying four guys to stand on Underwood Avenue and direct traffic. Today they were dressed as a milk carton, a lizard, a small building and a dancing horse. The dancing horse even had a tutu.

With everything going well at the slushie stand, Jack and Noah retreated to Noah's basement.

"Noah, why is your video game all dusty? I thought you were letting Dirk and Turk play it every week because they work for us."

"Nah, they gave it up weeks ago. They're spending all their free time trying to figure how to open up a skateboard shop. They figure if we can start a successful business, they can too."

Jack opened a new notebook, and he began to write as Noah read every movie idea the boys had recorded in the past five days.

"OK, let's see," as Noah shuffled through dozens of papers and candy wrappers. "Here we go. Jumping off buildings. Launching rockets. Disappearing like the wicked witch did in the Wizard of Oz. Have Stella lift weights or have a boxing match with a cat. Dress Henry up like a fire hydrant and see if any dogs notice. Blow up a..." Noah kept reading for over twenty minutes.

Some of the ideas were good, but most were really bad. Jack and Noah debated, argued, laughed, paced, picked their noses and did a bunch of other things for the next four hours.

"That's not a very funny idea, Jack."

"And you think wearing a dirty diaper on your head is hilarious, eh?"

"Well, it's got to be better than watching paint dry."

"Oh, come on! Everyone says that anything boring is like watching paint dry. Let's prove them wrong. Watching paint dry is NOT BORING!"

"Jack, we're talking about paint. You're getting too emotional. Step back from the paint."

"I'm sorry, Noah. I'm starting to think that if you try too hard to be creative, you end up super boring."

"That's gotta be what just happened. Maybe you're hungry. Here, I just found a piece of pizza in the toy chest," and he offered to Jack a piece of pizza that looked far too green to be healthy. Jack made a throw-up face.

"Fine, suit yourself. I'll eat it," and Noah did. Jack went outside for some fresh air.

Noah survived the green pizza, and Jack returned to the basement with more creativity. By the time the slushie stand had closed for business at 1:10 p.m., the boys had their movie script completed.

41 ACTION! – SATURDAY, AUGUST 9

Mr. Taylor had agreed to help the boys make a movie, but he would only help on the weekend. He had already taken four days of vacation this summer to help Jack, mostly with legal problems, and he needed to be at work, sitting at his desk, doing nothing but ordering people around. Jack hoped he could get that easy of a job when he was an adult.

Mr. Taylor, the boys, and half the neighborhood kids spent Saturday and Sunday filming the movie. For anyone who hadn't read the movie script, all the things the boys did seemed pretty unusual. Jack had decided that the movie needed to be a mixture of things that would be at the party – elephants, stunts, singing – and things that were just simply funny.

Mike Douglas, who watched movies all the time, didn't think the movie had any chance of being good. "Jack, I don't understand the plot," Mike said, waving the script in the air, "and all good movies are now shot in 3D. On top of that, none of my camp songs are in the film. The critics will hate the movie without my music." Jack ignored him.

In one scene, using a few camera tricks and a trampoline, Mr. Taylor made Jack's jump off a six-foot ledge look like he'd fallen off a three-story building. Jack landed safely, his fall cushioned by 500 moldy hot dog buns supplied by George's Gas Station. Greta had arranged for the hot dog buns; Jack was too busy to ask how she had gotten them.

Mrs. Taylor and Mrs. Patton learned the words to a popular Mandy Peters song, and then they moved their lips like they were singing the song. Mr. Taylor combined their video with the real song, and the moms looked (and sounded) like stars.

Henry dressed up as a bear cub and then acted like he was attacking Lauren. Once Lauren turned her dance moves into karate fighting, the bear didn't stand a chance. By the end of her scene, Lauren was tossing around an empty bear suit like a rag doll.

Greta and Delaney worked for three days straight to create a thirty-second cartoon on Greta's computer. The star was Banana Man, a bright yellow superhero who would beat up bad guys with his peel. If someone tried to escape, Banana Man would throw part of his peel ahead, causing the bad guy to slip and crash into trash cans.

"Why trash cans?" asked Noah.

The question annoyed Greta. "Metal trash cans are the noisiest thing on earth. Didn't you learn anything in first grade?"

Mr. Patton worked for a construction company, so he borrowed a cement mixer truck for the weekend. By using a rope and pulleys – and even more camera tricks – the video appeared to show Noah being shot out of the cement mixer and into the sky.

Meredith even got into the act. Mr. Taylor taped Meredith while she was moving her mouth and talking gibberish; she had just turned one, so she only knew a couple of words. Mr. Taylor wrote and sang a rap song that matched Meredith's mouth movements. It started out like this:

> "My diaper is stinkin'
> That's got me thinkin',
> I need to change my life!
>
> My binkie is crusty,
> It's making me fussy,
> My legs just want to dance!"

The end of the movie also included a brief mention about Omaha's birthday party on August 17 and the party's four charities. Jack and Noah were in the final scene, begging Charles Compton and Mandy Peters to come to the party.

Once the film was finished – all four minutes of it - the kids and parents argued about why each of them had the funniest scene. They could argue as much as they wanted, but Meredith stole the show. Nothing is as funny as a rapping baby.

On Sunday night, Mr. Taylor posted the video on YouTube.com. The four parents sent Greta the e-mail addresses for everyone they knew – over 1,000 e-mail addresses. Mr. Taylor alone had over 700 e-mail addresses on his work computer.

"Dad, how do you know over 700 people?" Jack asked, since he knew his dad just sat behind that big desk all day.

"I have a lot of meetings, Jack. Plus, I've been at the same job for over fifteen years. When you're as old as me, you know a lot of people."

"If you order people around all day and meet with 700 people, how can you do anything useful at work?" Jack was only eight, and he already worked harder than his dad.

"Go to college, Jack. I haven't worked hard since I got my college diploma."

Greta sent a link of the video to the 500 e-mail addresses on the summer camp list, plus the 1,000 e-mail addresses from their parents' lists, and asked everyone to forward the link to their friends.

42 GOING INTERNATIONAL – MONDAY, AUGUST 11

The YouTube website has a counter that shows how many times a video has been watched. On Sunday night at 8:00 p.m., Greta pushed the 'Send' button for her e-mail to 1,500 people. By the time Mr. Taylor went to bed at 10:30, only 5 people had watched the video. The next morning when Jack got up, the number of views was still stuck at 5. By 9:00 a.m. when Noah arrived at Jack's house, the video had still only been watched 5 times.

"Five times? That's horrible," groaned Noah. "Greta said all kinds of people would watch our movie. What did she say this morning?"

"Noah, today's a sleeping-in day for Greta. She won't be up until at least 10:00."

"Jack, you have to get her up now."

"Have you ever seen Greta when she gets up too early? She's meaner than a hungry eight-toed Nigerian sloth."

"Don't sloths just hang around in a tree for days without moving? How can a sloth be mean? And don't sloths have three toes, and come from New Jersey?"

"Fine, I'll get her up, but you'll have to explain it to my mom if I get hurt."

Jack knocked on Greta's bedroom door, and avoided stepping on dolls and laptop computers as he walked to her bed.

"Greta," he whispered.

"Why are you bothering me? I'm not taking appointments today." Greta was somewhere under her sheets.

"Um, Greta, you sent out those e-mails over 12 hours ago, and only five people have watched our video. Did you do something wrong?"

"Jack, unlike eight-year-old boys, I never make mistakes. I set up the e-mails to be sent out at 10:00 this morning when most people will be sitting at their computers. Hardly anyone reads their e-mail on Sunday night."

"But five people already watched it. How can that be if you didn't send out an e-mail?"

"Jack, how many times did we watch the movie last night before we went to bed?"

"I'd say about five times…"

"Exactly. Go away, I'm sleeping. Bother me again, and you can run the summer camp tomorrow."

Putting aside their disappointment, the boys retreated to the attic to keep planning the party, which was now only six days away. Noah had realized on Sunday night – when he was going to the bathroom – that portable bathrooms weren't on their checklist. Jack was shocked that they hadn't remembered something so obvious, and they decided at 11:30 to take a break to clear their heads.

They clomped down two flights of stairs from the attic to the first floor. They wanted to play catch, but Jack stopped to check the counter on YouTube before they went outside.

"Noah! Come here now!" Jack yelled.

Noah practically flew into Mrs. Taylor's office. "What? What?"

"Look at the number of views! It's gone from 5 to 612 since this morning!" Jack could hardly breathe, but Noah was causing such a ruckus that Mrs. Taylor sent them outside.

Jack tried to sneak a look at the computer when Mrs. Taylor called the boys in for lunch, but Mrs. Taylor wouldn't allow it. Finally, at 1:30, she gave the boys permission to check back on the computer.

"We're up to 2,500 views, Noah! We've got over 50 comments on the video – here's one from Hawaii … one from Japan… this guy's in Alaska!"

"Alaska! You mean we're world famous now?" asked Noah.

"Well, technically Alaska is in the United States, but I think Hawaii and Japan make us world famous, don't you?"

The boys headed back to the attic to do more work, but they couldn't stop thinking about the video. They returned to the computer at 3:00, and the video had over 5,000 views. By 4:00, they were at 7,000. When Mr. Taylor came home from work at 6:00, there were 11,312 views.

Their movie had become famous, but the boys weren't satisfied yet. They needed their party to be famous too.

📖 📖 📖 📖 📖 📖 📖 📖

Mrs. Taylor had planned a busy evening for the kids – eat, drag Stella on a walk, play catch, take an early bath, and in bed by 9:00. However, she got caught up in the movie madness too. She ended up ordering pizza, and the family huddled around her computer until bedtime.

16,532 views at 7:00.

23,863 views at 8:00.

37,386 views at 9:00.

And the kids still weren't in bed.

The views topped 50,000 at 9:52 p.m., less than 12 hours after Greta's e-mail had been sent. The boys had read over 800 comments about the video, and at least half of the comments were from other countries. Meredith was a star, and the party was on the map.

43 MEDIA BLITZ – TUESDAY, AUGUST 12

Mr. Taylor's plan to save his vacation days took another bad turn on Tuesday. He made it to his office by 7:00 a.m. – when the view count had been pushed to over 100,000, thanks to all the people in Asia and Europe who watched the video while America slept – but he had to head back home at 8:00 to help Mrs. Taylor.

The Taylor phone had begun ringing non-stop at 7:30 a.m., and then Mrs. Taylor's cell phone started chirping too. The national TV news stations – CNN, Fox, NBC, ABC, everybody – had been alerted to the video. By typing in the words "Omaha" and "party" on Google, a half dozen Omaha newspaper articles appeared, all talking about Jack Taylor and Noah Patton. The news stations wanted interviews. They offered to fly the boys to New York, Los Angeles or Atlanta just to appear on their shows. Mrs. Taylor told the callers that they could just fly themselves to Omaha if they wanted to talk to the boys so badly.

Mrs. Taylor was trying to answer phone calls and make breakfast, which was made more difficult because Henry kept yelling at her to get off the phone so he could hear his morning cartoons. Mr. Taylor was outside with Jack, still in his pajamas, while the local TV reporters played rocks, paper, scissors to see who got to interview Jack first.

In the middle of all this, Greta and Delaney were trying to get everything organized for the last day of summer camp. Movie stars or not, they were supposed to be at Elmwood Park in thirty minutes to host over 700 kids, and the three television trucks in the driveway weren't going to stop them.

📖 📖 📖 📖 📖 📖 📖 📖

Mr. Taylor allowed each local reporter five minutes with Jack before sending them all away. Mrs. Taylor informed anyone who called that Noah and Jack would hold another press conference at 2:00 that afternoon. She stayed home to answer the phone, but the rest of the Taylors and Pattons headed for camp.

Jack and Noah expected a hero's welcome when they arrived at camp, but the campers barely noticed them. However, when Meredith and Mrs. Patton got out of the car, the campers roared. If only Meredith knew why she was famous. On behalf of

Meredith, Mrs. Patton declined all autograph requests. After all, at her age, Meredith would rather eat a crayon than write with it.

The eighth and final camp held no surprises. The Amazing Arthur led a troop of eight clowns and magicians. The gymnastics team from the University of Nebraska performed one flip after another. After a three-week absence to get rid of his headaches, Ralph the soccer star returned for one last show.

The camp ended with the campers singing Mike Douglas' two biggest hits of the summer, "Aunt Gladice is a Radish" and "My Teeth Don't Smell (That Bad)." The campers cried, the counselors cried (especially the Christian book club members, who always seemed to be crying), and the Boy Scouts saluted. The camp had entertained over 2,500 kids in eight weeks, and the counselors hadn't lost a single one of them.

          📖 📖 📖 📖 📖 📖 📖 📖

The 2:00 press conference was held at Memorial Park for two reasons. First, it was a nice day, and Memorial Park is a great place to be on a sunny day. Second, the park was a whole mile from Jack's house, which was where Mrs. Taylor was right now, enjoying a little peace and quiet.

The view count for the movie at 1:30 p.m. was over 200,000. YouTube had placed the movie on its 'Most Popular' list, which led to even more views.

Jack, Noah, Mr. Patton and Mr. Taylor went to the press conference. Despite repeated media requests, Meredith and Lauren stayed home and took naps. Greta and Delaney were stuck at home counting the camp money (over $4,000), while Henry decided that playing basketball in the driveway was more fun than another dumb press conference.

Since this was the boys' second press conference – although the first one without an elephant – they were great in front of the cameras. They talked about the party and how they really wanted basketball star Charles Compton and singer Mandy Peters to appear. They explained how they had now raised over $15,000 in eight weeks, as if any kid could do it. But most importantly, they talked about the four charities they wanted to support. They planned to spend $15,000 on their party, and hoped to raise $40,000 more to give to the charities. The old goal of $20,000 was too low now.

The boys and their video were featured on every national news station that night. ESPN even had a story about Charles Compton and his connection to the biggest party in Omaha's history.

By 10:00 that night, well after the boys were asleep, the movie had been viewed more than 500,000 times. Mrs. Taylor unplugged all the phones in the house and went to bed. Being Jack's mom was an exhausting job.

44 PARTY EVE – SATURDAY, AUGUST 16

The video views topped one million by Thursday, August 14, and nearly every TV station in the United States had done some kind of story about the video and the party. The publicity was so great that Mandy Peters and Charles Compton both phoned the boys – yes, they actually made the calls, not their grandma assistants – to say that they'd be coming. In fact, Disney announced that it was sending Mandy to Omaha in a private jet with three other of its biggest stars.

When it became clear that all the money raised at the party was going to charity, the Taylor house was hit with a new wave of phone calls. However, these phone calls were from the non-scary clowns, the bounce house rental stores, the portable toilet company, and everyone else that was providing something for the party. Instead of getting paid for their services, they were now offering to do it all for free to help the boys reach their $40,000 goal. Even better, the 25 bounce houses grew to 50 bounce houses, and the number of clowns grew from 10 to almost 200 when the Shriners' clowns volunteered to help.

45 PARTY ON, DUDES! – SUNDAY, AUGUST 17

August 17 was a perfect summer's day, sunny with a cool breeze from the north. The day started early again for Jack and Noah – this time at 5:00 a.m.

"I didn't even know there was a 5:00 in the morning," said Henry, trying to rub the sleep out of his eyes. "When did they invent that?"

"No time for being lazy, kids," said Mr. Taylor as he ran down the stairs and into the kitchen. "The portable restrooms are arriving at the park at 6:00, and the 2-mile run starts at 8:00. We've got to mark the course with spray paint, set up the stage for the concert, and a million other things."

"When is the Pancake Man starting?" asked Henry.

"Nine o'clock," replied Jack.

"I'll see you at 9:00," Henry slurred as he stumbled back towards the staircase. "Stella is in my bed and she needs someone to keep her warm."

"Unfortunately, Henry, Stella already has enough fat on her body to keep herself warm. We have work for you." Mrs. Taylor knew that a five-year-old kid couldn't do much to help, but if she left Henry and Stella at home alone, the house might not be standing when she returned.

📖 📖 📖 📖 📖 📖 📖 📖

The Pancake Man began flipping pancakes promptly at 9:00. Noah had tried to stay overnight in Memorial Park so he'd be first in line, but Mrs. Patton wouldn't allow it. In fact, at 9:00 a.m., he was in the middle of picking up a few hundred paper cups that were left over from the 2-mile race. That didn't stop him from eating, though. Mr. Pancake Man had sent over five pancakes for Noah; two were already resting comfortably in his stomach, while the remaining three were underneath his baseball cap.

Uncle Bill, who was both a rancher and Jack's uncle, arrived at 9:15 in a big truck full of cows.

"Uncle Bill, are you sure it's safe to have cow races? I've never seen cow races on ESPN. I have seen bull-riding, and, um…"

"Don't you worry one bit, Mr. Jack. We have cow races in our town every summer, and hardly anyone ever gets hurt too awfully bad. But," and Uncle Bill whispered this so only Jack could hear, "you did arrange for an ambulance to be here just in case, right?"

"I did, Uncle Bill. In fact, there are about twenty firemen helping us today. It's a long story, but I got to know the firemen and policemen pretty well this summer. They have some great stories. Unfortunately, a few of them are about me."

"Oh, Jack, I've got a few stories too. Did I ever tell you about the time…"

"I'm sorry, Uncle Bill," Jack interrupted, "but I've got to go meet with the mayor. He says that someone important wants to make a surprise visit today."

"Run along, Jack. My cows and I will be fine without you."

📖 📖 📖 📖 📖 📖 📖 📖

Jack found Noah and they headed to the stage to meet the mayor. Along the way, Noah shared some bad news.

"Jack, I'm sorry, but it sounds like the airplane races aren't going to happen. I should have paid more attention to the races when they're on TV. They only do them over the ocean, and everyone watches them from the shore. Plus, there's some dumb rule that says that airplanes have to stay on the ground when someone important is in town."

"Who would be that important?"

"If I had to guess, I'd say Mandy Peters," replied Noah. "She's got her own TV show, she has a concert tour, and she's dating one of those famous brothers. Yep, she'd have to be the most important person in Omaha today."

Jack and Noah met the mayor behind the stage. Jack was surprised. Not only did the mayor want to make sure the boys had everything they needed for the party, but he also seemed smart, funny and nice.

"You're really nice, Mr. Mayor," offered Jack. "On the news, they always make you look like the bad guy."

"I was just going to say the same thing about you two," replied the mayor. "Thanks for throwing this party. I'm excited to be here – my favorite band, "Two Screws Loose," is playing – plus I have some great news. Someone very important is coming to the party. I just got a phone call from…"

"Jack! Noah!" The boys turned around and saw Henry running their direction. "One of Uncle Bill's cows got loose! We need your help!"

"Sorry, Mr. Mayor," Jack said quickly. "We'll see you later."
The boys dashed off.

📖 📖 📖 📖 📖 📖 📖 📖

The cow, appropriately named 'Roadrunner,' was eventually
caught after he ate two dozen pancakes and a tub of butter. Noah
thought he could have eaten more than Roadrunner, but there
was no time to waste before the 10:00 cow races began.

Adults could take part in one of eight cow races, and the
winner of each race advanced to the finals. The first seven races
were fairly uneventful, with all the cows circling an area about as
big as a football field. A problem arose in the last race, however,
as soon as it started. Jack and Noah heard a blood-curdling
scream as the 20 cows and 20 riders left the starting gate.

"Was that Mrs. Douglas?" asked Jack.

"To be honest, it sounded more like Crazy Luke," replied
Noah.

Or maybe it was both of them. Even though only adults were
supposed to ride the cows, Crazy Luke was seated on top of the
largest cow in the race, again aptly named Big Bertha, and he was
in the lead halfway through the race. Mrs. Douglas was trying to
catch up to Crazy Luke, but it was impossible. Not only was Big
Bertha exceptionally fast, but the race track was full of cow

manure. Mrs. Douglas was too busy dodging piles of cow manure to see Luke pass her, which was probably for the best. Crazy Luke was no longer seated on the cow; he was now standing on top of Big Bertha as if he were riding a surfboard.

Crazy Luke won the race by at least fifty feet. He was not allowed to race in the finals. He did visit the ambulance for a new pair of underwear.

📖 📖 📖 📖 📖 📖 📖 📖

The soccer tournament and concert both started at noon. While they were a few hundred yards apart, the music drifted over the soccer fields and made for what one mother later said was 'the most unique soccer tournament of her life.' Jack and Noah couldn't decide if that was a compliment. Of course, the bands playing were Omaha favorites such as the Burning Frogs and the Accordion Rock Band – not really the kind of music that Mandy Peters would sing. In addition, the soccer fields were in the same location as the cow races. While Jack, Noah and the firemen got most of the manure off the fields, there wasn't much they could do about the smell.

Slash Steven's motorcycle show began at 2:00, and it wasn't long before all the soccer players had wandered off their fields towards the motorcycle course.

"Your grandpa is pretty handy, Jack," commented Noah. "How long did it take him to build those two ramps for Slash?"

"He and Slash worked on it all day yesterday. I know Grandpa Dave can build anything, but…"

"But what?"

"You see how the support legs underneath the ramp are so shiny?"

"Yeah, I'm surprised they had time to paint the ramps."

"That's not paint. That's duct tape. My grandpa ran out of nails, so he started using duct tape."

"So, what you're saying is… we need to say a quick prayer for Slash?"

"Definitely."

The jumps went fine. In fact, Slash set a world record by jumping over 5 elephants, 50 Shriner clowns and two police cars that were between the two ramps. Slash hadn't planned to attempt a world record, but when the five elephants decided to move closer to the jump site, the clowns and police cars tried to stop them. Apparently elephants don't follow directions from clowns or police cars.

A basketball game featuring Charles Compton, a few of his NBA friends, and the Creighton University basketball team was scheduled to begin at 4:00. Unfortunately, just before tip-off, the boys heard a loud thumping noise, and then they and the crowd saw a large military helicopter headed toward the park. The crowd scattered, and the helicopter landed about fifty yards from the concrete basketball court.

Jack was mad. The basketball game was going to be the highlight of his day, and he was supposed to coach Charles Compton's team. He ran towards the helicopter yelling, "Move your helicopter!"

"Wait, Jack, wait!" Jack turned around and saw the mayor running behind him. "Jack, this is what I was trying to tell you earlier. Your surprise visitor is in the helicopter!"

📖 📖 📖 📖 📖 📖 📖 📖

The rest of the day was a blur, not just because of who was in the helicopter, but also because of how much Noah and Jack had to do. After the basketball game they had to present trophies to the winners of the strong man competition, introduce Mandy Peters on stage, thank all the volunteers, and pick up trash. There's a lot to do when 50,000 people come to your birthday party.

Mrs. Patton recruited about 50 high school kids to walk around with trash bags collecting donations. Since everything was free, including the elephant rides and the 10,575 glow-in-the-dark necklaces, the donations kept coming. It would take three days to count the money, and it would have taken longer without help from Rachel's entire sixth grade class. Three days seems like a long time, but when you've got $123,982 stuffed into 97 trash bags, it takes a while to organize it all.

46 THE BIRTHDAY – MONDAY, AUGUST 18

The boys slept in on Monday, but they were still tired when they met at Jack's house at 1:00 for their last meeting of the summer.

"What time did you get to bed?" asked Noah.

"I think it was 2:30. When we were leaving the park, my dad found about twenty piles of elephant dung, so we had to go find a shovel and trash can to pick them up." Jack made a squashed-up face.

"Hey, it can't be any worse than cleaning out the portable bathrooms. Dad tried to tell my mom that the porta-potty company has a high-powered cleaning hose, but she made me scrub every one of them. It's bad enough cleaning toilets when five people live in your house. Doing it for 50,000 people is pretty disgusting. People in Omaha need to aim better."

"You probably didn't feel like eating after that, huh?"

"Are you kidding? I forgot to eat dinner once the President showed up. We went to the House of Pancakes at 2:00 this morning."

"I thought the President would be taller," remarked Jack. "Still, did you think it was polite of Charles Compton to dunk on the President in the basketball game?"

"It had to be done, Jack. When the President made a three-point shot and yelled at Charles, 'This is my Supreme Court, and I have judged you,' Charles had to start playing for real. Mr. President sure was a nice guy, though. I'm glad the park was big enough for his helicopter to land."

"That was a cool surprise. Can you believe he wanted to ride an elephant?"

"Everyone wants to ride an elephant," observed Noah. "Which reminds me, that was first on the list of things you wanted to do on your birthday. Did you ever get to ride one?"

"No," said Jack, shaking his head. "I was next in line, but then Slash asked if I wanted to ride around the park with him. I couldn't pass that up. Plus, I'll have plenty of time to take an elephant ride when I'm nine."

"THERE WILL BE NO ELEPHANT RIDES!" Jack's mom must have been standing by the attic door.

Jack smiled. "Did you see my mom and dad on the elephant? The director of the Wilderness Preserve let them ride one of the elephants back to its transport truck. Mom told Dad she had wanted to do that since she was a little girl."

"Geez, ninety years is a long time to wait for something like that. I think my mom's dream was to clean 100 porta-potties." Noah couldn't get the smell of the porta-potties out of his head.

"So, Noah," Jack said as he pulled out his notebook. "We have to figure out what to do with all this money. Rachel's got a bunch of sixth-graders counting the money, but we think it's over $100,000."

"You were right all along, Jack. That's a little bit more than the $9,000 we had two weeks ago." Noah was enjoying his third breakfast of the day, picking pieces of a very flat granola bar from the inside of his sock.

"Yeah, you were right, Jack," said Greta, as she walked out of the attic bathroom. "I've officially taken your party idea out of the 'Dumbest Idea Hall of Fame.'" As she walked down the attic stairs, she added, "You're not in the Cool Brother Hall of Fame yet, but bringing Mandy Peters to Omaha was a good start."

Noah shook his head. "You'll never get into the Cool Brother Hall of Fame, Jack. My dad said that sisters turn into monsters when they become teenagers."

"I know. But you didn't hear about the other money."

"There's more?" Noah looked confused.

"Way more. Mandy Peters and Charles Compton each agreed to give $100,000, and the President gave me a check for $25,000." Jack waved the President's check in the air.

"Doesn't the President own all the money in the United States? I can't believe Mandy and Charles gave more money than him."

"My dad said that the President doesn't get paid that much. Charles and Mandy probably make more money in a week than the President does all year."

"So we're over $300,000? The four charities are going to get a lot of money."

"Actually, they're not," and Jack paused. "Our moms talked to the directors of all four charities yesterday, and they only want $10,000 each. The Humane Society said that $10,000 would buy enough dog food for two months, and the Wilderness Preserve director said that they had already collected over $60,000 because of our YouTube video. Anyway, after we pay those four charities, I figure we've got at least $250,000 to give away. On top of that, people all over the world are still giving money through Greta's website."

"Jack, school starts in seven days. Mom says my haircut will take seven hours, and we have to buy school supplies, and new underwear, and do all the stuff we do every year before school. I don't think we have time to give away $250,000."

"Relax, Noah. Mr. Dooley suggested we make our own charity, and the charity can spend the next year deciding how to give it away. I want Mr. Cousins – the guy from the supermarket who lost his job – to be the first person we help."

"And then Dirk and Turk's family? Their mom still doesn't have a job."

"Definitely. And then the people at the homeless shelter we always drive by. But we'll let adults do all that giving away stuff. Mom says we need to focus on school. She says the spelling tests in third grade are pretty hard."

"That reminds me, Jack. Happy birthday, Mr. Nine-Year-Old. What are you doing today?"

"Not one thing. But tomorrow – tomorrow is going to be a big day. Starting tomorrow, we'll only have six days before we go back to school…"

"That means we have to find something to do for six days, twenty-four hours a day," interrupted Noah.

"But don't forget sleeping and reading, and going to church on Sunday."

"Right, but we've got at least six hours a day where we've got nothing, absolutely nothing, to do."

"I say we start building a real time machine." Henry was still mad at Jack about the time machine joke.

"And then we should help Greta open her lawyer office."

Noah was sure that would be a huge moneymaker.

"Great idea. Let me get a piece of paper and we'll start... "

ABOUT THE CHARITIES

Camp CoHoLo held its first camp in 1985 at the Eastern Nebraska 4-H Camp thirty minutes from Omaha, Nebraska. 'CoHoLo' is an acronym for <u>Co</u>urage, <u>Ho</u>pe and <u>Lo</u>ve, the guiding principles behind the camp. Each year over 130 children with cancer and blood disorders spend four to five days at camp. The camp is entirely supported by volunteers, and over one-third of the overnight counselors are former campers. Visit <u>www.campcoholo.com</u> for more information.

The St. Stephen's Mission is, for simplicity, the name I created to represent several different homeless shelters in Omaha. I am most familiar with the Open Door Mission and the Sienna/Francis House, but all of the homeless shelters do wonderful work. These shelters are always in need of volunteers and donations, and I encourage you to support them.

The Nebraska Humane Society was founded in 1875 and is the fifth oldest Humane Society in the United States. For over 50 years, the Nebraska chapter served both animals and children, but it has focused only on animals since the 1940's. It provides education, gives sanctuary to animals, encourages adoptions and promotes responsible pet ownership. Visit www.nehumanesociety.org for more information.

The Nebraska Wildlife Shelter does not exist. Yes, I made up the whole story about the shelter. However, I had a good reason. I needed to find some elephants for the big birthday party, and there aren't many elephants wandering around Nebraska, especially ones looking for parties where they can give elephant rides. Zoos don't usually rent out their elephants, and you can never count on the circus to be in town when you need them. If you were me, you would have made it up too.

ACKNOWLEDGEMENTS

More than a dozen friends and family members read this book and provided feedback. Joanna Meysenburg, Jack's fourth grade teacher, read a late version of the book to her class and gave me the perspective of thirty 10-year-olds. She also led me to David Greenberg, an outstanding editor and author of children's books. David reminded me that nothing comes easy, whether it's writing a book or planning the coolest birthday party ever. If David had not prodded me to dig deeper, you would have never read about the exploding house, Inspector Kraznick or the boys' struggles over how to spend their money responsibly.

Other reviewers included Amy Peyton, Rachel and Melissa Slagle, Julie Richards, Beth Nodes, April Labedz, Shanda Hall, Janice Stultz, Audra Cavanaugh, Kim Craig, Connie Brown, Emma and Heather Gunn, Mary Drelicharz and Calla Pappas. I'm sure there were others, but you tend to forget a few things over five years. My dear mother, Betty Slagle, reviewed at least three different versions of the book and never complained.

I am indebted to Roberta Christensen, a much better and harder-working attorney than Mr. Dooley, who provided me with timely legal advice. I'm not sure that my book includes any intellectual properties, but she kept me on the straight and narrow.

Writing a book takes time. When you have a full-time job and a young family, writing a book takes time away from your family. A lot of time. Over a span of five years, my wife Jeana was extremely gracious in allowing me to work on this book on vacation days and nights at home when I should have been paying attention to her. She's one of a kind.

All of my children read the various versions of this book and, while they were not particularly tough critics, they were always positive in their feedback. As soon as the first draft was finished, Jack asked the question that he has now repeated dozens of times: "Are you going to get it published?" Yes, Jack, I am going to get it published. This book is my gift to Henry, Greta and you. I hope the three of you dream big dreams and have the coolest lives ever.

ABOUT THE AUTHOR

Jay Slagle is the proud father of Jack, Greta and Henry, as well as Stella the basset hound and Lily the rabbit. In case you were wondering, the dog and the rabbit do not get along. Jay started writing this book as a way to keep Jack and his best friend Noah interested in reading during the summer between second and third grades. The book turned into a family project, with Mrs. Slagle reading chapters to the kids every night before bed.

Most of the stories in this book are make-believe, but the spirit and enthusiasm of the children are entirely true. If Jack, Noah, Greta, Delaney and the rest of the gang decided to plan the coolest birthday party ever, Jay is pretty sure they could do it. And that, my friends, would be a pretty cool story.

Made in the USA
Charleston, SC
09 November 2013